No Perfect Affair:
Renaissance Collection

No Perfect Affair:

Renaissance Collection

Charmaine Galloway

www.urbanbooks.net

Urban Books, LLC
300 Farmingdale Road, NY-Route 109
Farmingdale, NY 11735

No Perfect Affair: Renaissance Collection
Copyright © 2017 Charmaine Galloway

ISBN 13: 978-1-62286-612-0
ISBN 10: 1-62286-612-6

First Trade Paperback Printing December 2017
Printed in the United States of America

10 9 8 7 6 5 4 3 2 1

This is a work of fiction. Any references or similarities to actual events, real people, living or dead, or to real locales are intended to give the novel a sense of reality. Any similarity in other names, characters, places, and incidents is entirely coincidental.

Distributed by Kensington Publishing Corp.
Submit orders to:
Customer Service
400 Hahn Road
Westminster, MD 21157-4627
Phone: 1-800-733-3000
Fax: 1-800-659-2436

No Perfect Affair:

Renaissance Collection

by

Charmaine Galloway

Also by Charmaine Galloway

Girlfriends Secrets

The Secrets They Kept

Tyree's Love Triangle

Golden

Heaven's Cry
(short story)

Jordan's Confessions
(short story)

My World, Through My Eyes
(poetry)

And Check Out Charmaine's Young Adult and Children's Books

Girl Talk

Finding The Princess Within

I Love Myself As I Am

Mommy's Little Superhero

Acknowledgments

First and foremost, all praises go to God. Through you, I'm blessed, I have peace, and I'm whole. Your love, grace, and mercy have kept me. I would've lost my mind a long time ago if I didn't believe in your Word. Thank you for blessing me with a talent to write stories that will, hopefully, inspire and entertain others. Lord, you are my everything.

I would like to thank my children, Shayla and Shayne, for adding so much joy and fulfillment to my life. They are the reason I follow my goals, goals I've set because I want them to know that it's okay to reach for the stars and to accomplish whatever their heart desires.

I would like to thank Racquel Williams, my publisher, for allowing me to be on her team and for believing in me and the work that I put out. We have been friends since the beginning of our writing careers, and I'm so proud to be on her team. Shout out to all of my sistas and brothas on my team; we are family, and we rock together. Let's get it!

I would like to thank all the family and friends that have supported me on my journey toward accomplishing my goals. I love you all.

I would like to thank my editor, Milan, who has been here from day one. I am blessed to have her in my corner, giving me her honest criticism. I know whatever you tell me is only to make me a stronger writer. I would also like to thank, Lisa Muhammad, for her assistance with her honest criticism and proofreading my work.

Acknowledgment

Thanks to all the authors and to all the people that have supported me on social media by sharing my post and listening to my blog talk radio interviews. Thanks to the newspaper editors, online magazines, online blogs, blog talk radio, and online Web sites that interviewed me and promoted my work. Thanks to the book clubs that have chosen my work for their reading selection.

I would like to thank all of the amazing readers for giving my books a chance. I appreciate you all from the bottom of my heart. I love hearing your thoughts after you have read my books. I greatly appreciate the feedback. When I read my reviews, I am so glad that you enjoy the stories that I pen. You all inspire me to keep writing.

Many blessings,

Charmaine Galloway

1

Sasha

I love my husband, but he was driving me straight to the crazy house. All he wanted was to get me pregnant. But I didn't want no kids, and if he found out that I was on birth control, he probably would have killed me.

I could smell bacon frying and knew my husband was trying to pamper me by cooking me breakfast, but I wasn't feelin' it. I was lying comfortably on my black silk sheets, not wanting to get up because my head was throbbing from the Cîroc I drank the night before. I knew I shouldn't have gone out with Melody and Asia. Every time I went out with them, I always drank too much and paid for it the morning after. But this time, as soon as I got home last night, my husband and I got into it.

"Babe, what I tell you about coming home drunk? We trying to have a baby. You need to let loose on the alcohol. If you can't handle your liquor, then I'm not going to allow you to go out with yo' irresponsible cousins," he snapped at me as if I were his teenage daughter.

"Wait a damn minute! What do you mean you not going to allow me to go out? You need to dismiss yo' self with that bull. I may have had a few drinks, but I ain't drunk. You are not my daddy, and you are not going to sit there and tell me where I can and can't go," I spat as I took off my heels. I could feel the heat coming through my pores.

"Babe, I didn't mean it like that. I just want to make sure you stay healthy, you know . . . so we can have a baby," he said with compassion.

"You need to stop stressing me out. I'm not able to have any more kids!" I shouted as I walked away from him.

I had tried to convince him that after my miscarriage, my body wasn't strong enough to produce another baby. I really wanted to tell him that there would be no baby. But it didn't matter how many times or the different ways I told him; he wouldn't listen to me.

"Sasha, don't say that. I can feel it. We have been trying hard, and I know you will be pregnant pretty soon. And I can't wait to be a father." He grinned and took me in his arms. Then he continued, "Let's make love right now."

As horny as I was, I didn't want to make love to my husband. He turned me off because he concentrated so hard on making a baby that he didn't pay enough attention to me. He didn't make me feel that passion that I needed to feel while making love to him. There was no connection or affection. All he did was gently slide his shaft inside of me because he thought I would break, pump a few times, explode in me, smile, and then roll over and pray that when we woke up I would be pregnant. He had a stash of pregnancy tests in the nightstand, and he would beg me to pee on the stick the day after he had his five minutes of fame.

It was not always like that. We had been married for two years, and I used to make passionate love to my husband. He definitely knew how to work my middle, and he knew how to keep my juices flowing. But after I had that miscarriage last year, he was devastated, and he hadn't been the same since.

The only thing on his mind was having a baby and making sure that I kept my body healthy so I could get pregnant and carry the baby full term. I took the miscarriage as a sign that maybe it just wasn't time for me to have a baby. If left up to me, we didn't need any. We had enough running around my family. If I wanted to goo-goo and gaa-gaa with a baby, I could pick up one of Asia's kids. And the best thing about that was that I could drop their behinds right back to their mammie.

Asia was my cousin, and the girl had more kids than I could remember. She had three, or maybe she had four. Hell, I don't remember; I lost count. And they all looked different. They were all different races and had different daddies. That girl should've been ashamed of herself. And she treated her kids so wrong.

She did take good care of them. She gave them what they needed to survive, but she was so mean to them. She would call them out of their names and holler at them all day. Well, she was nice to her daughter, Angel, because she was her favorite, and she let everyone know that.

Asia, at times, couldn't stand me. I didn't know why because I ain't never done nothing to her. I think she's jealous because I had a husband, and I didn't have any kids to stress me out. And she had a bunch of kids and couldn't pull a good man, let alone a husband, if her life depended on it.

My other cousin, Melody, all I could do was shake my head when it came to her. She was driving herself crazy because she was in love with a man that apparently didn't love her. She was in such denial of being his side chick. Yes, I hooked her up with Rodney a few years back. I thought they could have fun together, but she done went and fell in love with him.

I told her many times not to get all up in her feelings with every man she met, but, naw, she had to get all emotional and attached to the "D" that she didn't know what to do with herself. But I rooted for them. I hoped Rodney would get his stuff together.

"Bebe, your breakfast is served," my husband, Jonathan, said, pulling me from my thoughts. He walked into our spacious bedroom with one of my good bath towels wrapped around his waist and a tray with pancakes, eggs, bacon, and a red rose on it.

Oh, Lawd! He was trying to be romantic so he could pump his wannabe-baby-making-sperm in me after he fed me breakfast. "Thanks, Jay." I plastered on a smile.

"Anything for you, beautiful." He smiled and kissed me on my cheek. "Did you get a chance to take the test this morning? Last night was great. I think I might have hit a home run," he said, rubbing his hands together.

Sometimes my husband could be so corny, and I wanted to slap him upside his head when he said the dumbest things. "Yes, I did. It was negative," I lied about taking the test. I knew it was going to be negative.

"Well, soon as you are done eating, we can try again." He stood and let his towel drop to the floor. Then he put his hands on his hips like he was Spider-Man or Superman—one of those damn superheroes, and said, "Daddy is ready."

Well, I'm not.

I almost choked on my food as I glared at his limp penis. He just didn't know, but there wouldn't be no damn baby coming out of me. And I was tired of his boring sex.

2

Melody

"Mel, I love spending time with you, but I look at you as only a friend and not as my woman."

"What! What are you trying to tell me?" I stammered over my words as I swallowed the dry lump in my throat.

"Babe, I really enjoy spending time with you, but I want to make sure we are on the same page." Rodney had a serious expression on his face as he looked into my eyes. We were seated at my glass kitchen table. He had just finished cooking us breakfast after a long night of passionate lovemaking.

"What's up, baby?" I put a piece of turkey bacon in my mouth. I was curious about what he was going to tell me.

"You my boo," he said, not really answering my questions.

"I know I'm your boo; we've been together for two years," I reminded him.

"We have been friends for two years, not together" he replied, looking down at his plate. He knew he was wrong; he couldn't even look me in my eyes.

I gave him a scorching look. "You have to be kidding me. All the time we've shared together, and all the sex we done had, and now you telling me that I was nothing but your sex partner?" My words were sharp.

"I enjoyed the time we spent together, but I'm not ready to be the man you need. Give me some time so I can work on myself. You deserve the best," he placed his hand on top of mine.

I snatched my hand away because I didn't want him to dare touch me. "You should have told me that before we had sex. You should have told me that before I introduced you to my family. I brought you around my daughter like we were a happy family." It felt as if I was going to pass out. I stopped to catch my breath and then continued. "And all this time I meant nothing to you. I didn't mean enough to you to be your woman," I spat. My heart hammered in my chest. I wanted to get up and wrap my two hands around his neck and strangle him to death.

"Mel, I love you," he pleaded.

A single tear fell from my eye. "Dismiss yourself with that bull!" I shot daggers at him. "How could you hurt me like this? Wait a minute, is there someone else? Is that why you're saying this now? You want to see someone else?" Sweat trickled down my face, I was heated with anger. "No, don't answer that 'cause most of the time that's what it means when a man comes out and says we are 'just friends.'" My vein throbbed at my temple. I stood up from of my chair and got right in his face. "Get out of my house before I do something I regret!"

That was two years ago, and there wasn't a day that went by that I didn't think of Rodney. He hurt me deep down in my soul. I wondered why he didn't want me to carry the title of being his woman. He was the man I wanted to marry. I wasn't going to be his side chick. But he had never told me there was another chick. Maybe he did just want to get himself together to be the man I needed. But to me, he was perfect the way he was.

"Melody," Sasha yelled my name from across the club, snapping me from my thoughts.

"Hey, boo," I sang to her when she walked over to me. I was sipping on a strawberry margarita on the rocks and, honey, I was feeling myself. I knew I was looking cute wearing a black, form-fitting dress that hugged all of my curves just right. I showed just enough cleavage to keep it sexy and classy. I didn't waste my money on all those high-priced designer clothes. I got my dress from Dots, my favorite place to shop for women's accessories, clothing, and shoes. I knew I was looking hot.

"Hey, Mel, you lookin' cute. I know who you must be looking for wearing that dress. That's right, girl, do yo' thang. 'Cause when he sees you, he's gonna want to tap that tonight. You haven't been out in a while, and this is the way you're supposed to look when you make a comeback." Sasha smiled, and then put her hand up to give me a high five. She continued, "I'm surprised he ain't all up in yo' grill right now." She turned her head and looked around to see if she could see Rodney.

"Who y'all looking for?" Asia asked when she walked in the club and gave me a one-armed hug.

"Girl, nobody important. What's up?" I tried to change the subject from Rodney because when his name was spoken, my insides started to tingle. I took another sip from my straw as I eyed Asia down. She was wearing a tight, low cut, black shirt that showed all her belly rolls and some dark jeans with a pair of red, open toe stilettoes.

"What's up is you need to get that bartender's attention so I can order a drink," Asia demanded. I got Asia's Grey Goose with cranberry, and she sat in the middle of Sasha and me. We sipped on our drinks and bobbed our heads to the music that thumped loudly through the speakers. We all flirted with the fellas and allowed them to buy us more drinks, even Sasha with her married behind.

Asia, Sasha, and I were cousins, and we had been inseparable ever since our childhood years. We were around the same age, and we got along great. Don't get me wrong, we got into it sometimes, and we didn't agree on hardly anything, but we were family, and that's what made our bond strong.

Asia was our cousin through marriage. My uncle Charles married Asia's mom Rosa when we were kids. Asia's mom would spoil Asia and my uncle when we were young. Whatever they wanted, Aunt Rosa would bend over backward for them. My uncle kept a job, but Aunt Rosa would still take care of him by giving him all the money that she earned. I think that rubbed off on Asia because when we became adults, she began to have issues with allowing men to use her for her money. She had developed low self-esteem dealing with the men in her life, so much so that she had three children, and they all had different daddies.

Sasha was my mother's sister's daughter. Like Asia, Sasha had her issues too. First of all, Sasha and Asia were always getting into it, and I had no clue why. Sasha was in a miserable marriage, and she wouldn't tell her husband, Jonathan, that she had been unhappy ever since her miscarriage. Her husband wanted to have children, but she didn't. I guess Asia's three demon seeds scared her straight. Those were my li'l cousins, but those heathens were off the chain. It seemed as if Asia was a gremlin; every time she got close to water, she popped out another baby.

Whenever Sasha was stressed out about what was going on in her home, she would work her stress out on the slot machines at the casino. Then she would be calling me saying that she was more stressed out because she blew her money. But lately, she had stopped going to the casino and started going to the clubs to drink hard liquor.

I loved my cousins, but they had their issues, and I'm sure my issues weren't as bad as theirs. All I needed to do was get Rodney to understand that I was the only woman that he needed in his life.

As I sat at the bar, I hoped I wouldn't bump into Rodney because if I saw him, I knew I might've become weak to his sexual desire. I thought about him daily, and I yearned for his touch. It's been two years since I had been sexually involved with any man, and I wanted to save myself for that man that I wanted to marry. I was trying to stay strong because I wasn't going to keep letting him play with my emotions. But I just couldn't keep him off of my mind.

How did I get here? I remember when I met Rodney at this very club, a few years ago. He'd told me that he had a girlfriend, but his relationship was on the rocks. I kept it cool because I didn't mess with other women's men. My cousin Sasha introduced me to him because he told her he had been peeping me out when I came to the club, and he wanted to meet me.

Rodney was undeniably a catch. He was tall and wore a size fourteen shoe. His hair was cut in a tight fade that complemented his smooth, caramel skin and tapered goatee. His swag was like no other, and the brotha was confident with it. You know what they say about tall men with big feet. And the saying was so true when it came to Rodney.

I took his number, and we talked on the phone, getting to know each other very well. We always saw each other at Club Headliners, and every time I bumped into him, he would be in my grill all night like he didn't have a woman at home. We would talk, dance, and he would buy me and my girls drinks for the whole night. That went on for a few months.

Then he came to me and told me that he and his girl broke up. He said that they just wanted to go their separate ways. I told him I was sorry to hear that, but that was a lie. Because all the time we spent together at the club and all the conversations we had on the phone, I was ready to be his woman. But I wasn't going to let him in that easy. He was going to have to work for this.

He had just gotten out of a relationship, and I wasn't going to be his jump-off chick. I didn't work that way. If we weren't in a relationship, we were not going to be having sex. I told him that it was cool for us to go on dates since he was a single man. We went to the movies and dinner every other night. We were so inseparable at the club that people thought that we were a couple. That went on for a whole year. I enjoyed the attention that he gave me because I knew the ladies wanted him, but I was the one with him. He was well known around town, so he would speak to chicks when we were out, but they definitely knew that he was into me. I finally had sex with him, and it was amazing. I thought that was when we made our relationship official. I introduced him to my daughter, and she loved him too.

"Mel, look over there. Yo' boo just walked in the club," Sasha said, snapping me from my past and into the present.

I glanced over toward the entrance, and there he stood, all six feet three inches of fineness. When he smiled, I melted like hot butter. He looked good, even if he had on a white tee and sweatpants. I hurriedly turned my head back the other way. I didn't want him to see me looking at him. I wanted him to come over to me and flirt with me like he always did. I wanted to play hard to get.

I was on my fourth margarita, and I took it to the head. I could feel my insides tingle. Tonight it wouldn't be too hard for him to get me. I wanted him so badly I made myself sick thinking about how he made me feel behind closed doors. I loved him, and I wished that he would see that I was all he needed. I wanted him to want me like I wanted him, and not just sexually. But I was human, and I needed to get laid. I was going to make him love me. Just looking at him walk through the doors of the club sent butterflies to my stomach as waves of euphoria filled my body.

Lord, please give me strength to keep my legs closed to Rodney Hampton.

3

Asia

I've had my share of men in my life. I loved me some black men. My mom once told me, once you go black, you never go back. I kind of followed in her footsteps. My oldest son's father is white, but my last two children's fathers are black. My mother was exactly right, because I would take a black man, either light chocolate or dark chocolate, it didn't matter to me; they were all packing. The blacker the berry, the sweeter the juice is what I learned from Tupac, one of the illest black rappers out here.

When Sasha, Melody, and I kicked it at the clubs, people were surprised when I told them we were cousins because Melody and Sasha are black, and I'm a blond-haired, blue-eyed white chick, with no ass at all. My mother married into their family, and they treated me like I was blood.

One thing I always envied growing up was that Melody and Sasha had nice plump behinds; not too big but just right. Every boy in our high school would tell them how nice their figures were. But the boys seemed to always skip past me and act like I wasn't even there, with my belly protruding over my jeans and my jeans sagging over my flat behind. I'd always been on the chubby side ever since I was a baby. I get it from my mother. She was big boned, and she loved to cook.

I was so happy when I saw a commercial advertisement on TV about butt pads and the waist trainers. I asked my mother for her credit card and called the number on the screen and ordered the garments. I couldn't wait for the package to be delivered to my doorstep. My body was banging just like Melody and Sasha's. With my belly rolls tucked away and the butt pads, I was looking bootylicious. Beyoncé had better watch out.

"Angel, if you don't get your funky, boney feet off my couch, I'ma break both yo' ankles. I ain't raised no animals, so stop acting like one!" I yelled at my middle child. People have told me that I'm a mean-spirited person to my kids, and, in general, but they are just sensitive. My kids were giving me gray hairs, and I was only thirty-four years old. What had I gotten myself into? I loved my three kids, but they were bad as hell. And none of their daddies were around to help.

My oldest child, Joey, had a father that had gotten married and was playing house with his wife and her children. My daughter Angel's father, Steve, was in prison, and my baby girl, Alexa, had a father, Delroy, that had just moved out of town. He said he needed to get away because his life was too stressful in Ohio. But let the truth be told, he moved as soon as he was told by the courts to pay child support.

I had some sorry baby daddies. Truth be told, I couldn't stand Joey or my baby girl Alexa 'cause they both looked like their good-for-nothing pappies. But, Angel, we got along because she looked just like me.

I tried raising my kids the best way I knew how, but I was starting to lose it. With me being a full-time Realtor and mom, something had to give. My doctor said that I may have been going through postpartum depression. She wanted to prescribe me some pills to help me calm down so I could function better, but I wasn't about to become addicted to popping no pills. Those doctors killed me. Their remedy to all their patients' problems was to prescribe some pills that would make them crazier with all the darn side effects. Those prescriptions had every side effect that you could think of. They should've just written on the bottle, "This Medication Will Kill You Slowly."

"Joey, what the heck is going on in there? It sounds like you in there tearing up when you are supposed to be cleaning up," I yelled at my twelve-year-old son who was in the kitchen washing dishes.

"Sorry, Ma, the glass slipped out of my hand. I'll clean it up."

"You're the clumsiest doe-doe I know. Ya darn right you gonna clean it up," I snapped.

It seemed like every week I was buying new dishes because if my kids weren't breaking them, they were throwing them in the garbage. If they kept on playing with me, they would be eating off of paper plates and Styrofoam cups. At times, I couldn't stand my son. He was so lazy. He didn't want to do nothing but sit around and play his video games. And on top of that, he was starting to look just like his stupid daddy. I despised that man for leaving me and getting married to a chick he met on BlackSinglesMeet.com. He wasn't even black. I don't know how that happened. Maybe he was lying about how they met.

My phone rang. I looked at the caller ID. It was my middle child's father calling me from prison. Steve was getting out soon, and I knew he wanted to come and shack up with me and my kids. I did want my kids to have that father role model, and he was Angel's father, but I was seeing someone else, and I didn't really want to be bothered with him. Plus, I didn't know how he would feel about me having another baby while he was locked up.

He told me he was hurt and would have to just deal with it. But he was saying that over the phone. I wanted to see how he would be in reality when he got out.

"Hello," I spoke into the receiver. I sat and listened to the operator; then I heard Steve's voice.

"Hey, Asia. How are you and the kids doing?" He sounded all pitiful.

"We good, how are you doing?" I knew that was a dumb question since he was locked up and all.

"I'm cool. I'll be getting out in a few weeks. I can't wait to see you, Angel, and the other kids."

"Yeah, Angel misses you."

Steve had been locked up for two years, and our daughter, Angel, was six years old. That's all she talked about, how much she couldn't wait to see her dad again. I didn't take her to see him in prison, but I allowed her to speak to him over the phone.

"Asia, I know I wasn't right when I was out, but when I come home, I'm going to be a good man to you. I'm going to find me a job, and I am gonna hold you down like you been holding me down since I've been in the joint."

Yeah, yeah, whatever! He was talking that jail talk, about how good it was going be when he got out. Jobs were hard to come by. He would be lucky to even find a job that paid minimum wage.

Steve was a good father and a good man, but I had fallen out of love with him. I'd kinda gotten bored with him. He wasn't spontaneous. I was. I wasn't the type to bite my tongue. He was. They say that opposites attract, and we were definitely opposites. We had our daughter from a one-night stand, so I just dealt with him being the father of my child. But since he was getting out soon, he swore up and down that he loved me and always did. He said he wanted to make it work between us. I just didn't know how to tell him I was seeing someone else.

Yes, I had been putting money on his books every week and making sure he had the stuff he needed, hoping that we could be together when he got out. But about a month ago, I met Lance, and when I tell you the brotha was fine, that was an understatement. His body was toned like no other, and when he smiled and showed off his perfectly white teeth, he would mesmerize you from miles away. Maybe because that's all you saw were his teeth in the dark because he was so dark, but that's the way I liked them. He was smart and intelligent, and I had a lot of fun with him. Did I forget to mention that the sex was magnificent? Just thinking about him made my toes curl.

"Asia, you still there? We only got one minute left," Steve said, breaking my thoughts.

"I'm still here," I stuttered, trying to get Lance out of my mind.

"Are you gonna be happy to see me?"

"Yeah, I guess," I said, not enthused at all.

"Okay, babe. I'll see you in a few weeks. Give Angel a kiss for me and tell Joey I said hello. And, Asia, I love you," he said before the call was disconnected.

When I hung up the phone, I realized that he never acknowledged Alexa, my daughter that I conceived while he was locked up. I had to break it to him as soon as he got out of jail that this wouldn't work. I may have yelled at my kids, I may have said bad things about their dad in front of them, I may have even called them out of their name a few times, but I would never put any man before my children. If Steve couldn't come to grips with me having three kids instead of the two I had when he went away, then he was gonna have to step. But then, if he did accept Alexa, what would I tell Lance? I didn't know what I wanted, I was so torn.

4

Melody

The sun shined brightly through the large window that was on the side of the bed. I turned and looked at the man that was sound asleep next to me. All I could think about was the long night of intense lovemaking we had.

"Hey, sexy," he crept up from behind me.

I turned my head to the side, and there he stood, his hypnotic cologne filled my nose, and I wanted to dive into his arms. I acted like I didn't see him when he entered the club. "Hey, Rodney. How long you been here?" I smiled seductively.

"I just got here. Can I have a hug?"

Being in his presence made me shake in my bones. I twirled my seat around, reached out to him, and wrapped my arms around his neck. He wrapped his arms around my waist and planted a soft kiss on my cheek. My whole body shivered from the touch of his lips. I needed to get it together. I needed to control myself before I exploded with ecstasy.

"You are looking good enough to eat," he licked his lips.

I rolled my eyes and smiled. "Stop it." I playfully shoved his arm. He knew how to turn me on with his words.

He got the bartender's attention, told her to get him a Long Island Iced Tea and get me and my girls whatever we wanted. "You want something to eat?" He asked, his eyes danced when they looked into mine.

Stop looking at me. You are making me hot. "Yes, some chicken and fries, please." *I could feel sweat running down my chest. That was not sexy at all. I needed to go cool myself off.*

"Okay, I'll go order it." *I watched him as he walked away. I was filled with glee, like a teenage girl on her first date. The man did something to me, and I couldn't control myself.*

Sasha, Asia, and I chitchatted and listened to the music while we sipped on our drinks. Rodney stood right behind me the whole time like the hulk, whispering sweet nothings in my ear.

"I miss you so much." *He blew hot air in my ear and on my neck. He knew exactly what he was doing.*

I looked him in his eyes and gave him a looked that said whatever.

"No, I'm serious. I want you." *He was in my ear again. His words had my insides tingling. I tried to stay in control of my emotions, but I seemed to be losing the battle.*

"Rodney, you already know how I roll. I am not going let you play with my emotions any longer," *I said seriously, talking over the music, looking dead in his eyes.*

"Mel, I don't have a girl. I want you. I miss you. Babe, I love you. Can I please have you?" *He rubbed his hand up my thigh discreetly.*

He had done enough. His touch was what I wanted at that moment, and my mind was made up. I told my girls that I would call them the next day; then Rodney and I left the club.

"Are you driving?" *I asked.*

"Nope, my truck is in the shop," *he said.*

He followed me to my car, and I pulled off. "We going to your house?" *I asked.*

"No, my bathroom is messed up. My pipes are backed up," he said.

"What that got to do with me coming over?" I asked.

"Let's go to your place," he blurted out.

"My daughter is there."

"Well, let's go to a hotel."

We pulled up to a hotel, and he asked me to go in and get the room because he was too tipsy. He gave me the money to pay for the room. When I got back in the car, I saw the light on my phone. No, he wasn't looking through my phone. I smiled, knowing that he was checking up on me. I didn't say a word about the phone. "Do you have protection?" I asked.

"Nope."

I sighed, then drove to the gas station to get some condoms. We were finally in the hotel room, and I knew what I wanted wasn't right. I had been doing so well. I had been celibate for two years, and I promised myself that I wasn't going to have sex again until I found that right guy. But deep in my heart, I wanted Rodney to be the right one.

So in my mind, I thought once I gave him the good lovin', he would want to commit to me, and we would be together. We had been knowing each other a long time, and he knew I was a good woman. I had a good job, I took care of my business, and he knew how I felt about him. So what else did the brotha need? Nothing, because I was going to give him whatever he wanted, without asking. I knew that he cared for me too.

After I put my purse down on the chair that was in front of the bed, Rodney came up to me and kissed my lips slowly. I wanted to melt in his arms. We stood in the middle of the room kissing for a few seconds; then he removed his lips from mine. He planted wet kisses on the left side of my neck, and then the right side. He then *cuffed my butt in his large, masculine hands. My panties instantly became moistened. He unbuttoned the few buttons on the back of my dress; then he slowly pulled the dress down below my breasts, then below my waist. As he did that, he looked at my body as if it was a feast that he was about to dig into.*

"Babe, your body is so sexy," he panted.

My heart beat at a fast pace because I was excited about what was about to go down. We had been down that road many times, and every time he knew exactly how to satisfy my needs.

"I want you so bad," he said right before he kissed me below my navel. Then he went lower until he reached my hot spot. I moaned.

After he came back up for air, he laid my body down on the bed and tore his clothes off as if they were on fire in his rush to get to me. I watched as he placed the condom over his swollen manhood. I shivered when I felt the tip of his manhood rub against my inner thigh. I inhaled as he slid in slowly, stretching out my insides. His thrusts were slow, just how I liked it. He knew what I needed, and he gave it to me. And then we climaxed together, forcing me to cry out his name as a single tear fell from my eyes. The tear did not come from a sad place. The man had me mesmerized, and I loved him with all my being.

"Mel, you hungry?" Rodney asked, pulling me from my thoughts.

"Yes," I said as I lay my head on his chest and listened to his heartbeat. I didn't want to leave. I wanted to just lie in his arms. I yearned for his touch. I wanted that moment to last forever.

After we got dressed, we went to a small café and ate breakfast. After we ate, he asked me to drop him off at his mother's house. When we pulled up, he gave me a kiss, told me he loved me, and that he would call me later. I felt good. He didn't tell me we were a couple, but he told me that he loved me, and he was only making love to me. So I felt that in a few weeks or maybe a month, we would make it official. He just needed a little time, and I didn't mind giving that to him.

5

Sasha

Lately, it seemed like Melody, Asia, and I had been going to Club Headliners every weekend. I knew Melody was going to meet up with her boy toy Rodney. I wished he would get his act together because she was a good woman, and I knew how much being over thirty without a mate was really stressing her out. I knew he was a playboy, but dang, I thought by now he would have grown out of that stage of his life. He was hitting forty.

I knew Asia enjoyed going out to get away from those little hellions of hers. And she did enjoy tossing back a few shots of tequila like it was Kool-Aid. I felt sorry for her at times. She walked around with low self-esteem because she was overweight in her midsection. She would complain about how her clothes fit her. She needed to stop worrying about her flaws and get it together. The first man that said she was cute, she took him in and catered to him like she was his sugar mama. I told her that she shouldn't be spending her hard earned money on no man, but when I told her that, she would just blow me off and tell me to mind my own business. She had a good job; she was one of the highest-paid Realtors in the area. There were plenty of women that had flabby midsections because they had children. But I wasn't going to let her worry me.

***

I looked in the mirror at my five feet five, 150-pound physique. If I should say so myself, I looked amazing. I took a bottle of Avion Silver Tequila out of the cabinet that my husband had stashed away and sipped on it as I got dressed. I decided to rock the long sleeved, skintight, thigh-length Versace dress that my husband purchased for me last week.

I enjoyed going out because my personal life sucked. The only action I had in my life was writing short erotic stories that I was thinking about publishing in the near future. Asia and Melody read them and said they were hot. I wished I had the courage to show my husband so we could re-create the scenes in our bedroom. But I knew it would hurt his feelings if I told him that lately, our lovemaking was pretty boring.

Jonathan spent most of his weekends away playing golf tournaments. I couldn't stand golf. Even when he tried to explain it, I got bored listening. My husband and I worked at the Chrysler assembly plant. Jonathan had been there for seven years, and he was a plant supervisor. I had been working there for four years, and I was an assembly operator. I liked my job, and I made good money. I received my BA in communications, but it was so hard to find a good-paying job, even with my degree. I always wanted to be a news broadcaster, but my childhood dreams never came true.

Jonathan and I met on the job. We dated for two years; then we got married. We didn't have a big wedding because I'd never been the one to want to plan a huge fairy tale wedding and spend all that money for one day. Plus, I was pregnant with our first child. I did put pressure on him to marry me before I had the baby because I had seen so many women having babies out of wedlock and their baby daddies leaving them to care for the babies by themselves. I wasn't going to be left with no hollerin' baby to raise alone. And I wasn't going to have no baby daddy. We flew out to Las Vegas and were married in a small chapel.

I fell in love with Jonathan because he truly knew how to treat me like a queen. He wined and dined me, respected me to the fullest, and pampered me like a real man is supposed to pamper his woman. But it wasn't just about him spending all his money on me; he was a gentleman. He pulled out my chair and opened doors for me. He was loyal, and he loved me for who I was. Where I'm from, that type of man was hard to come by. He was definitely a catch, and I caught him.

Four months into our marriage, I had a miscarriage. I was five-and-a-half months pregnant, and it was a girl. I was hurt, but Jonathan was devastated. He named the baby and kept all the ultrasound photos. We had a small home-going for Johnasia, and he visited her grave every month. I tried to delete her from my memory because she wasn't full term anyway.

Melody thought I was harsh when it came to how I felt about the baby I lost. Maybe I was that way because I never had a mother to love me. My mother was crazy, and she didn't want me. I thought that having that miscarriage was a blessing because I would never be a good mother. And if I ever told Jonathan what I had to go through as a child, he probably would understand why I was taking birth control so I wouldn't get pregnant ever again. But I just couldn't come to grips enough to tell him about the birth control.

My phone rang, pulling me out of my thoughts. "Hello."

"Hey, boo, are you ready? I'm around the corner." It was Melody.

"Yes, I'm ready. But should I drive my own car? You know when you see Rodney you are going to want to leave with him," I giggled, but I was serious.

"He told me he wasn't going out tonight. He's watching the game."

"Okay, whatever. Here I come," I said as I slipped on my Versace heels.

That was the first time Rodney wouldn't be there. That dude didn't miss a night out at the club. It was like his second home. So he must have been with another chick. I just hoped my girl didn't put all her emotions in that dude again, 'cause I didn't want her to be crying in my ear if, and when, he broke her heart.

The club was packed like always, and the music thumped through the speakers, playing one of my favorite songs by Rihanna.

"Pay me what you owe me. . . . Don't act like you forgot." I sang out the lyrics as I bobbed my head to the beat.

The club was very basic. It had a nice-sized dance floor, a rectangle-shaped bar that was in front when you walked in, and a few tables lined against the walls. There was also a pool table by the dance floor. They served food from the kitchen in the back. We went there frequently because that was one of the only clubs that checked your ID at the door and had police officers on-site. We were too grown and sexy for the other clubs that let the young crowds through the doors with no security on deck.

We walked over to the bar where I ordered Cîroc with cranberry juice. I turned my head and saw Asia talking to this fine brotha. He was slim, chocolate, with a baby face and a low haircut. His eyes connected with mine. I quickly turned my head and took a sip of my drink.

"Hey there, Ms. Lady," a baritone voice said from behind me.

I was caught off guard. I turned around to see where the voice came from. It was the guy that Asia was talking to. "Hello," was all I said.

"My name is David. I saw you walk in with Asia, and I asked her if you were single," he said, looking into my eyes seductively.

He stood about six feet, and his muscles popped out of his shirt as if he had just left the gym. "And what did she say?" I asked, looking into his sexy, light brown eyes.

"She told me to come over and ask you." He smiled, showing the gap between his two front teeth. It was sexy on him.

"Well, I'm married," I said, turning my head back to take another sip from my drink.

"Why do all the fine woman have to be taken?" He shook his head in pity.

I smiled but said nothing. My song was on. It was "Slow Motion" by Trey Songz, and I started to dance in my seat.

"Can I at least have this dance? I see you like this song."

I smiled and nodded my head. He took my hand and walked me to the dance floor. I loved dancing. I tried to dance for my husband in the bedroom, but he would tell me to stop because he was so lame.

I gently pushed David out in front of me so he could watch me as I slow grinded my body and rolled my hips for him while my hands were over my head. He licked his lips as he watched me, then took a napkin from his pocket and wiped the sweat from his forehead. He slowly reached for my hand, and I walked closer to his body as I continued to slow grind. His cologne smelled so good. Then he placed his hands on the small of my back. His touch was gentle but strong.

"Damn, baby, you are so sexy. You didn't even tell me your name." He blew his hot peppermint breath in my ear.

I didn't say a word. I turned around and arched my butt against his manhood. I could feel his hardness. He then gripped my hips with his hands, and I continued to grind against him. Any other time if a man would put his hands on me while I danced, I would've push his hands away, but not this time. I had yearned for this type of touch for a while. My mind had zoned out for a few minutes. It was like I was reliving one of the scenes in my short story. The main character was alone at the club with her man, and they were dancing; then they got naked, and they made love in the club. I had to come to grips with myself before I started taking off my clothes. I was in the mood to do whatever. I wanted to be free. I was into my character's mind, the one that I wrote about in my erotic stories. I wasn't myself. The song went off. He pulled me close, my chest collided with his. He asked, "Can I have you tonight?"

Without even telling him my name. Without thinking. With no hesitation, I said, "Yes." I wanted him, and I didn't care that I belonged to someone.

6

Asia

Last night was crazy. I couldn't believe that Sasha left the club with David. What in the heck was this world coming to? Ain't she married? Melody had the nerve to catch an attitude because I let her leave. I sat back and allowed my mind to replay last night.

"Where's Sasha?" Melody asked as she looked around the club.

"She just left." I rolled my neck and tooted my lips, but I was smiling on the inside. I could feel it. It was about to go down, and I was going to be front and center when Ms. Goody Two-Shoes crumbled once the spotlight was on her.

"With who?" Her eyes were wide like saucers

"With an old friend of mine."

"Who?" she spat.

"David," I barked. She needed to calm down, acting like Sasha was her child.

"Was she tipsy? Why would she leave like that?" She questioned me like she was the FBI.

"I don't know. I wasn't babysitting her. Maybe you should have. Why you asking me all these questions? I'm leaving," I said, and I walked toward the door. Melody followed behind me. She ranted and raved about why I let Sasha leave. She tried to call her phone, but the girl didn't answer. We then got in our cars and went our separate ways.

I knew David from college. We had the same sociology class. We both were going to school to receive our BA in business administration. We became really cool. One night after I attended a frat party, he saw me walking alone, and he stopped.

"Why are you walking out here alone at two o'clock in the morning?" He sounded like the police.

"I'm good. My dorm is just right there." I pointed to the huge building that was about twenty feet away.

"Hop in. I'll give you a ride."

I got in his car, and we ending up talking for a while. We had a few things in common, so he invited me on a date the next day. I went, and we had a good time. I spent the night at his dorm because his roommate wasn't there. We had sex that night and a few times after that. I didn't fall in love or nothing. I just looked at it as having a little fun. After that, we kind of grew apart. It was nice seeing him at the club. I haven't seen him since college. When I saw him, he was so interested in knowing who Sasha was. I told him her name, and I also told him she was married. Obviously, he didn't care because he took her home with him. They darn sure didn't go out for coffee or a burger. And they *definitely* didn't go to Sasha's house.

I really didn't care for Sasha that much. Yeah, I loved her because she was my cousin, but I couldn't stand her. But it was only right to stay cordial with her. She married my first love. Melody, Sasha, and I went to the same high school, and so did Jonathan. Jonathan and I graduated the same year. Even though Jonathan and I never dated, he was the first boy to ever kiss me. Sasha knew that he was my first crush. When she told me that she had gone to Las Vegas and gotten married, I wanted to knock her teeth out of her mouth. We were all at dinner, and that's when she made her announcement.

"Hey, ladies, I brought you here to tell you something," Sasha said full of glee.

"What? You and Jonathan having a baby?" Melody said with excitement.

"Yup," she grinned and continued. *"And we got married."*

"What?" I blurted out.

"When? And why weren't we invited?" Melody spat.

We were both furious with her.

"It was the spur of the moment. We flew to Las Vegas and got married in a small chapel. It was just the two of us."

"Why would you marry him, Sasha? You knew he was my first crush."

"Girl, are you serious? That was in high school. We are grown now, and we've been together for a few years. Can you get over the past and just be happy for me?" Sasha hissed.

I was silent, but that moment, I had to catch my breath. It was like she stabbed me in the heart.

From that day forward, I had to look into Jonathan's eyes at every family gathering because he was married to my cousin. Sasha had broken the unspoken rule. You should never go behind yo' girls and have a relationship with a man they fell for first.

Before she walked out of the bar with David, I tried to warn her that I had him first. But she just waved me off like I was a fly buzzing in her ear.

"I didn't know she was going out like no slut. The girl has a husband at home." I shook my head with a devious smile on my face. I guess payback's a mutha.

7

Sasha

I told Asia to tell Melody that I was leaving the club, and I would be cool. She glared at me as if she wanted to say something, but I just walked away. I had a feeling that she was going to tell me that I shouldn't leave the club with a man that I didn't know. But right now, nothing mattered to me. I was on cloud nine, and I was going to do what my mind was set on doing. I was in a place where I wasn't thinking about my husband, my vows, or my morals. I wanted to be spontaneous. I wanted to be free. I always wanted to live on the edge, but my husband told me no. I hoped that tonight my dream would come true.

David and I walked out of the club, and he guided me toward the parking lot where his car was parked. He pushed the button on his key fob, and the lights to a CTS-V Sedan Cadillac blinked off and on. "The only way I'm getting into that car with you is if you let me drive." I was fierce with my words.

He looked into my eyes, smirked, and said, "All right, Ms. Lady, you can drive." He gave me the keys, and we got in. I drove out of the parking lot to our destination.

I pulled into Walbridge Park; then I drove down by the river and parked where there were no streetlights. I was tipsy from the drinks that I had at the bar. I'm glad we made it safely.

"We are about to get it in at the park? You *are* a little freak, huh?" He smiled seductively.

I didn't say a word. I got out of the car and sashayed toward the front of his vehicle and sat on his hood. The stars were bright, and the sound from the water pushing into the rocks was soothing. He followed me. He opened his mouth as if he wanted to say something, but I placed my finger to his lips. "Please don't say anything, David. Just do me. Take me now and take me hard." My words must have sent fire through his blood. He grabbed me by the back of my neck, pulled me close, and kissed me forcefully. He then lifted my dress over my head and quickly removed my bra and panties, leaving nothing on but my stilettos. He devoured me. He feasted on me. He drove me insane while tasting my whole body with a sexual hunger that I felt all the way to my toes. I enjoyed him more, knowing we were outside on the hood of his car. I allowed him to do whatever and however he pleased as the night wind blew through my hair.

When he was done exploring my body with his tongue, he stood up, got a condom out of his pocket, and took it out of the wrapper. I watched him roll it over it his shaft, and I was pleased at what I saw. He then took my hand and pulled me to the edge of the hood of the car. He gripped my butt in his hands. I wrapped my arms around his neck, as he slid his manhood inside of me, and my inner muscles clenched him. I moaned as I looked into the dark sky. At that moment, something fierce and overpowering tore through him, and like a jackhammer out of control, he thrust me hard, quick, and deep. The deeper he went, the louder I screamed. He growled. Our bodies were completely naked and wet with perspiration as I dug my nails into his backside. We kept going until we both climaxed at the same time. I had never in my life felt so good. So free. So sexually pleased. He had blown my mind, and I had enjoyed every minute of it. I was out of breath as I searched for my clothes. I wished we could have gone another round, but I had to get control of myself.

"Damn, babe, you sure know how to turn up." He smiled smacking me on my butt.

I exhaled, then blew out the air from my lungs. I was on ten, and I wasn't ready to come down. I walked to the passenger's side of the seat and sat quietly, trying to calculate what had just taken place. He got in the car and drove me to my house. I know that showing him where I lived was a very stupid thing to do, but it was four o'clock in the morning, and there was nowhere else he could take me.

"I'm married, and I hope you can respect that we can never do this again," I said bluntly, looking into his sexy, light brown eyes. I had never cheated on my husband in the past, and I hoped David wasn't the stalker type. I hope he was mature enough to respect my wishes.

"I respect that, but if you ever want to have another spontaneous night like we just had, please don't hesitate to give me a call." He winked at me and put his business card in my purse. I got out of the car and strutted into my home, the home I shared with my husband.

I walked into the bathroom that was adjacent to the master bedroom and pulled all my clothes off. I turned on the shower and got in. As the hot water pellets hit my body, I exhaled, and then breathed out slowly. My body was still on fire. What a night. What had I just done? Was I crazy? I just had crazy sex on the top of a car of a man that I didn't even know. A man that didn't even know my name. I was a character that I developed in my short story, and I loved bringing her to life, even if it was only for one night. Then I let out a giggle and said, "Damn, being her felt so good." I grinned like a teenage girl crushing on a guy. I didn't feel dirty; I didn't feel like a slut. I was just a woman that had a little fun getting her back blown out.

I wished my husband would allow me to be open and free like that with him. I wished my husband would go hard like David did instead of making love to me so delicately like I was going to break if he was a little rough with me. I frowned at the thought of how badly he wanted a baby. I sighed at the thought of him finding out that I wasn't going to have any kids, that I didn't want any kids. I didn't want to be in this marriage if things didn't get any better, if he didn't stop begging me for a baby. If he only knew that I wasn't going to get pregnant because I was faithfully taking birth control pills, he probably would no longer want to be in this marriage. I didn't know how much longer I could keep this from him. I didn't know how much longer I could keep faking that I enjoyed making love to my husband.

8

Melody

Rodney and I were back in love again. We had been going out to dinner and making passionate love every other night. He told me that he was not with anyone but me, and I knew he was ready to commit and be in a long lasting relationship real soon. He knew that I wasn't going to stick around if he wasn't a one-woman's man. I loved the time we spend together, and I couldn't keep him off my mind when we weren't together. And when we were together, we couldn't keep our hands off of each other. Sex with him drove me crazy.

Every time we spoke on the phone, he would tell me he loved me, and at first, I blew him off. I didn't want him to think that I was giving into him so easily. But then, every morning he texted me good morning, and every night he would text me good night. He would also check on me in the middle of the day, telling me he was thinking of me and that he loved me. At first, I blew him off, but then, he had once again stolen my heart, and I started telling him I loved him back.

My phone rang, and I searched my purse for it. My heart beat at a fast pace when I saw it was Rodney.

"Hey, babe, what you doing?" he said in his deep and sexy voice.

"Hey, you. It's funny that you called. I just rode by your house. I was going to stop by, but I saw a car in your driveway. I figured you were kicking it with the fellows," I said.

"Oh, I'm not at home."

"So whose car is in your driveway?" I wanted to know.

"Just friends." was his response.

"Friends?" I was becoming irritated because it seemed that this conversation was about to be all bad.

"Yes, she lets me drive her car when I need it. But, Melody, you don't have to worry about her, trust me," he said calmly.

I walked into the kitchen and leaned against the counter because my knees got weak. My daughter was in her room, so I tried to talk quietly. "She?" My heart skipped a beat. "What do you mean I don't have anything to worry about? You got a female's car parked in your driveway, and you are not at home?" I spat. Now I paced the ceramic tile floor.

"Yes, babe, calm down. She's staying with me for a little while, but I'm hardly there. We've been cool for a while, and she's going through hard times. She sleeps on the couch. We are not together, I promise. You don't have nothing to worry about," he pleaded.

"I can't believe you're doing this to me," I said and hung up the phone because I didn't want him to hear the tears in my voice. I couldn't believe that I had fallen for him again. I had been driving past his house, and I had seen the car parked in his driveway several times, but I thought one of his boys was letting him drive their car while his car was in the shop. I had no idea it was a chick's car. I was pissed.

She was staying in his house when he supposedly wasn't there. The tears came down my face. Then I thought for a second. No wonder he took me to the hotel instead of going to his house. But he told me his bathroom was messed up. "Why me, Lord? Why do I have to keep getting hurt? What have I done to deserve this?" I wiped the tears and went to check on Rayn. She was in her room watching TV. I didn't want her to walk in on me with me crying . . . crying over a sorry man. I wished I didn't fall for him so hard. I was too old for this. Too old to keep letting a man use me for sex. Too old to not be in a committed relationship. I needed to talk to someone because I was so hurt. Rodney kept calling me back, but I didn't answer the phone. I called Sasha.

She picked up the phone, and I cried in her ear. "Melody, is that you? What's wrong?" she asked very concerned.

I wanted to speak, but I couldn't get my words out because I was sobbing uncontrollably. My heart ached. I tried to catch my breath.

"Melody, please tell me what's wrong."

"Rodney . . . played me again," I stuttered. I could hear Sasha exhale. "Girl, I thought you was dying or something. What he do now?" She was nonchalant.

"All this time we have been kicking it, he got some trick living with him." Telling her brought back memories. So every time I made love to him, he went home to her.

"Girl, you need to kick him to the curb and stop going back to him. He ain't ready to settle down." She hissed like it was her in the predicament.

"I am so done with him. I thought if I gave him another chance, he would see that I am the woman that he needs." I cried some more.

"Mel, you need to dry your tears and get over him. He has hurt you too many times. He's crazy to be kicking it with you, taking you out, and he got a chick in his bed."

"Well, he said they ain't sleeping together."

"And you believe that?" She sucked her teeth.

I didn't know what to believe. I was just sick and tired of being sick and tired.

"Girl, if you can't keep the relationship y'all got without getting your emotions involved, then you need to move on. But I know you're looking for love, so it's hard for you not to get your feelings involved."

"He kept telling me he loved me. Why would he do that? He needs to just leave me the hell alone," I said as I sat down at the table. I rubbed my throbbing temple.

"He probably do love you, but he's just not ready to settle down yet."

I needed to get myself together. Here I was acting like a teenager crying over a stupid guy. In the past, if I found out I was being cheated on, I would walk away from the relationship with no turning back. But with Rodney, I didn't know how to just let him go and not give him another chance. He has broken my heart in the past, and he continues to break my heart. Why do I allow him to have such a tight hold on me?

"Mel, are you still there?" Sasha said, snapping me out of my thoughts.

"Yes, I'm still here," I moped.

"Don't let him keep pulling you down. He's fine and all, but he ain't worth it."

"Why you hook me up with him?" I hissed playfully.

"Girl, don't put that blame on me. I warned you, but you let him get yo' cookies; now, you all in love with the D." She laughed.

"It's so hard for me. I'm tired of meeting new men, and they end up being losers. I figured why not just deal with the men in my past," I explained.

"Because the men in your past got issues too. *That's* the reason they are in the *past* and *not* in your present," she smirked.

"Ugh, I'm just going to be single for the rest of my life."

"Girl, stop moping around. Your time will come when it comes," she pacified me.

"I'm glad I called. I needed to talk to someone. Girl, he's still texting me saying that he loves me."

"If that was me, I would keep spending his money, and I would call him when I wanted him to sex me down. Girl, you know you was all cranky when you weren't getting you none, but now that he's been tappin' that, you've been in a good mood."

"Girl, shut up," I laughed; then I continued. "Hold up. You talking about *me* getting some. What happened to *you* last night? Why did you leave the club with that stranger?" I wanted to know.

"Girl, it wasn't nothing. I had a headache, so he took me to get something to eat, and afterward, he took me home." She was clear with her words.

"Girl, you better stop getting in the car with strangers. I don't want to see a picture of you on Nancy Grace."

"Whatever," she replied, and we both laughed.

We said our good-byes, and I told Rayn to get ready so we could take a ride. I thought it would be a good idea to go to the mall. I needed to shop and buy a nice outfit to wear, so the next time I went to the club, Rodney would be mad that he messed up a good thing.

9

Asia

"Babe, you are looking good tonight," Lance said as he looked me up and down.

"Thanks, you ain't looking too bad yourself," I smiled and kissed him on the lips. The waiter had just walked us over to our decorated table. We were at a nice Japanese restaurant downtown. Lance complimented me again on how I was looking. I had picked him up from his house, and when I walked in, he told me that I looked too good for him to not get a taste. I didn't think that he was gonna yank me in his house and take me straight to ecstasy while I tried to balance myself against his living-room wall. But he did, and I enjoyed every bit of it. Now, thirty minutes later, we were sitting across from each other about to have a nice dinner.

"Do you know what you want?" I asked. Yes, I was paying the tab. I didn't mind doing that, especially after he just took real good care of me.

"Um, yeah," he replied as he scanned the menu.

When the waiter came, we ordered wine, and then our meal. I had been spending more time than usual with Lance because Steve was going to be getting out of jail tomorrow. I had not told either one of them about the other. I was torn, and I didn't know what I wanted. I mean, I loved spending time with Lance. He was sexy and all that, but I hated when he had to work. He was a truck driver. Sometimes he would be gone for days at a time. During the time he worked, I would get bored and miss him a lot. But I didn't complain because he had to make that money.

Lance and I had met at the grocery store. We were both in line to buy some fresh fish, and he was standing in line behind me.

"What's up, pretty lady?" he said softly, but his voice was still deep.

Was that every man's pickup line? "Hello," I said. He then asked me what type of meat I was buying. I thought that was very rude to be all in my business, but I told him anyway because he was gorgeous, and he smelled so darn good. I had to turn around and look him in his dark eyes. Then my eyes traveled down to his lips. I just stared at him as he talked. I watched his plump lips form the words that he said. And I couldn't help but to notice his bulging biceps through his shirt. After our conversation about the foods we enjoyed, he gave me his number, and we talked on the phone a few times; then he invited me out on a dinner date. And the rest is history.

"Ya know, Asia, lately, I have really been enjoying our time we spend together," he said, breaking me from my thoughts. He lifted his fork to his mouth.

"You know what, Lance? I have been enjoying myself with you also. You are so naughty, and I love it." I gave him a seductive smile.

"Girl, you just want me for this wood I carry," he smirked.

Hell, yeah, is what I wanted to say. "Babe, you know you do me right under the sheets, but you know I like the way you make me feel, no matter what we are doing." I ain't gonna lie. I did have some weight issues. I could stand to lose a few pounds, but Lance never made me feel uncomfortable with the extra weight I was carrying.

On the other hand, Steve had complained about my weight in the past. He would make little jokes, telling me that I wouldn't get no smaller eating and sitting on my behind all day. But since he had been locked up, he has been really pleasant with me and telling me that when he gets out, he is gonna be the man he needed to be for me and the kids. Melody said that was just jail talk. But I really wanted to be with him because we had a child together. I knew that having three kids by three different men wasn't the wisest thing I've done in my life. That's the reason why I wanted Steve and me to work out. But I would have to hold on to Lance for a while, just to see where Steve's head was really at once he was home.

Lance and I have been dating for six months. He had never met my kids. I didn't play that. I may have had a lot of relationships in the past, but I rarely brought men around my kids. I've heard so many horror stories about men molesting their girlfriend's children. I would have to kill a mofo if they even *thought* about touching my kids. Whenever I'm in a relationship, the first thing I tell a dude is that I have three kids and that my house is off-limits. If he wanted to court me, then we would have to find other places to kick it. Then I would add in a little joke, "If you ever want to meet my kids, rent the movie *BeBe's Kids*. Yes, they are all up-and-coming actors. They got their own movie." The men would laugh, but they didn't know I was dead serious.

"Babe, thanks for dinner. The food was delicious," Lance said, snapping me from my thoughts.

"Yes, the food was great here. This was my first time here," I said as I swallowed the last bit of my shrimp stir-fry.

"Don't you want to come and spend the night with me tonight so I can have my dessert?" Lance asked as he grabbed my hands from across the table.

That didn't sound like a bad idea, but I had to pick up Steve early in the morning, and I knew if I stayed with Lance, I wouldn't have the energy to get up on time. "I'm sorry, but I'm going to have to take a rain check." I poked my lip out and continued. "Remember I told you I have family coming in from out of town? I have to pick them up from the airport in the morning," I lied. It took me weeks to think about what I was going to tell Lance about why I wasn't going to be spending much time with him. I had no clue what I was going to tell him.

The kids were all geeked up when I told them I was picking up Steve, especially Angel. She really missed her dad, and I prayed that he would come out and be the father that he promised her he would be. I didn't want him to break her heart. I had faith in him because he was a good father, but he would always run the streets. However, he told me that he would look for a job and make his money the legal way this time.

"Asia," I heard a voice yell my name as I was sitting in my parked car in front of the Madison Correctional Institution. It was a two-hour drive, and I had driven a hundred miles an hour to get here on time. I turned my head to see Steve walking toward me with a bag containing all his belongings. I smiled and walked toward him.

He dropped his bag, lifted me up, and hugged me as my hair blew in the wind. "Girl, you are looking good." He smiled; then he kissed me hungrily.

"If you don't put me down . . ." I said after we unlocked lips. It felt as if he was going to drop me.

"I'm so happy to see you." He hugged me tighter.

"I'm happy to see you too." I smiled at his excitement.

"Where are the kids? You didn't bring Angel with you?" He looked through the car windows.

"Nope. They're at home waiting on you," I said as I walked over to the driver's side door to get in the car.

"I like this new ride you got. So, this is what the new Invader Lexus SUV looks like. This is sweet." He grinned like a boy with a new video game as he drooled over my car.

As we drove, he looked out the window, amazed at the changes of the scenery, like he'd been locked down for ten years. I wanted to ask him why he was so excited. Ain't much changed in two years. But I left him alone because I knew he was just happy to be from behind those walls.

"I picked you up a few things from the store yesterday," I said, breaking the silence.

"Aw, thanks, babe. I know in the past you would spend a lot of money on me, and I want you to know I appreciate that. But this time around, I'm going to take care of you. I'm going to keep me a job. I might not make as much you make, since you got a degree, and all I got is a high school diploma, but I'm going to get what I can get so I can help with everything." He was serious with his words as he looked in my direction. I just kept my eyes on the road. He continued, "I'm going to be the man I should have been before I went to prison. I've learned a lot from people in the pen. The things that I learned most was to be there for the people that had been there for me when I needed them. To never take life for granted. I met dudes that had life without parole. They would never have that quality time with their kids again. And to be the best father that I can be. I want to be a good man so my daughter will know what type of man she should deal with when she gets older."

My heart fluttered. I was touched by his words. It really seemed like he was going to be a changed man. I just sat back, drove, and listened to him talk my ear off the whole way home about how he was a changed man.

10

Sasha

Today had been a long day. I had to work overtime, and my feet were killing me. I couldn't wait to get home, take my shoes off, lie back, and read a good book. When I walked through the doors of our ranch-style home, I heard the sound of Marvin Gaye singing "Let's Get It On" in the background. Oh my Gawd, I hope my husband wasn't lying on the couch butt naked waiting to have sex with me. That has happened many times before. I told him he needed to give me a warning or something. The last time he did that, I walked through the door with Melody. She hasn't been over my house ever since. Don't get me wrong. Jonathan has a nice body, but who wants to see someone else's husband butt naked standing at the front entrance screaming out "Surprise!" with his cowboy boots on with Maroon 5 singing "Animals"?

"Welcome home, baby," my husband, said snapping me from my thoughts.

I turned and looked at him. "Uh . . . hey." I was at a loss for words. What was he up to? It was nice to see that he was fully clothed.

"I have a surprise for you." He smiled suspiciously.

I opened my eyes wide in shock and wondered what he was up to now. I had a dream not too long ago that I came home and my husband had called himself surprising me with a newborn baby that he had adopted! I stood there and hoped that bad dream hadn't come true.

"Why are you looking like that?" he asked as he took my hand.

"I want to know what's going on," I said softly. I looked into his eyes and walked slowly as he pulled me toward our spacious kitchen. I was so thrown off, that I hadn't smelled the aroma coming from the cooked food that was prepared nicely on the kitchen table. My husband had made a candlelight dinner for me, and there were a dozen red roses placed in a vase in the center of the table.

I smiled broadly and said, "Honey, this is beautiful. Thank you." I passionately kissed him on his lips. Without a word, he grinned as he pulled my seat out. I sat down; then he scooted me up to the table. While the music played in the background, he fixed my plate. He made baked tilapia, fried shrimp, garlic mashed potatoes, garlic bread, and broccoli. The food looked delicious. Jonathan was a great cook, and this was not anything new. He loved pampering me.

He sat beside me and said, "It seems like lately we haven't been spending enough time together. So I wanted to make this meal for you, and after you are finished eating, I have something else for you." He looked into my eyes and smiled jauntily at me; then he took my fork and fed me my dinner. Why was he so darn happy? I wondered. His face was going to crack from all the smiling he was doing.

When my plate was empty, he walked me to our master bathroom, where the jetted tub was filled with water. He turned the hot water on to heat it up; then he took my clothes off, one piece at a time. First, he unbuttoned my blouse and tossed it gently to the side; then he unzipped my jeans, pulling them off slowly. Why couldn't he yank my clothes off, smack me on the butt, and make love to me on the bathroom sink? When he grabbed my hand, he snapped me from my thoughts. He helped me as I stepped into the tub. I wanted to slap his hand and tell him I knew how to get in the tub by my damn self. He then got on his knees and took my sponge, lathered it up, and he wiped me down as the water from the jets messaged my body. I was full and relaxed. I wanted to close my eyes and fall asleep right there.

"How does this feel?" He squeezed the sponge, and the warm water ran down my back.

"It feels really good," I answered. My head rested on the back of the tub. He lifted my leg and washed my foot.

"I'm glad you're enjoying this because I wanted your body to be relaxed. Because I feel really good about tonight. I think tonight will be that night when you will become pregnant with our baby." His eyes brimmed with joy.

"Ugh," I sighed loudly. "You just messed up the mood," I hissed. I got out of the tub and searched frantically for a towel to cover my body.

"What's wrong, Sasha? What did I do?" His voice cracked as he followed me to the bedroom.

"Why can't you just stop pressuring me about having a baby?" I shouted.

"What?" He was stunned.

"I wish you would stop thinking so hard about putting a baby in me every time we have sex. I wish that you would devour my body like you are a wild animal, and I'm your prey," I spat at him through narrowed eyes.

"What?" He looked at me confused, like I was speaking another language, and he had no idea what I was saying. Well, to him, that *was* a language that he didn't know, but I wished he would learn. Did I have to go purchase some XXX videos for him to watch?

"When we make love, I wished you didn't treat my body like it's a damn delicate rose petal. I wish you would take me in your arms and handle me roughly. I'm tired of the slow and boring lovemaking sessions we have. I need a change," I demanded, and I waited for his response.

He paused for a minute as if he was trying to take in the words that were just thrown at him. "What has gotten in you?" He looked at me through squinted eyes. His body was tight as he stood directly in front of me.

I saw that I was not getting to him. "Never mind. I'm going to bed." I huffed and turned my back toward him. I was frustrated. I grew up listening to my aunts talk about how men should take the lead. I wasn't about to sit there and tell my husband what he needed to do to satisfy me. He's the man, and I wanted him to take control and give me what I needed.

He tightly grabbed hold of my arm and said, "Don't you walk away from me. I need you to tell me where this is all coming from." His voice was stern.

"Our sex life has been the same since we've dated. How come you can't do things out of the ordinary? Things that will excite me? I want you to turn me on. Put this fierce flame out that has been burning inside of me," I said as I posed for him. Then I put my hands on my hips, and I grinded those hips.

"What are you trying to say? I don't satisfy you anymore?" His voice was low, and his face was stained in sorrow.

Duh! I could see that my words were like a bullet straight to his heart. But I needed to get this of my chest. "I'm not happy. I wish you would stop thinking about having kids and make love to me like you want *me*, and not a baby. *I* have needs, and they are *not* being met sexually."

"Sasha . . . I thought you *wanted* to have a baby." He sat on the edge of the bed as if he no longer had the strength to stand.

"Since when?" I snapped. He was beginning to sound like a broken record, which irritated me even more. Was he *still* talking about a damn baby?

"Since we lost . . . Johnasia." It looked as if he was about to cry when he said her name.

I didn't try to comfort him. "I never gave you a reason to think that I wanted to become pregnant again. I knew that you wanted another child. I didn't want to hurt your feelings, so I just listened to you. But I never told you that I wanted any more children."

"Are you seriously telling me that right now? You know I always wanted to have kids. Now, you telling me you don't want one, and you telling me you haven't said anything because you didn't want to hurt my feelings?" He got up and paced the floor.

"I'm sorry, Jonathan." I held my head low in sadness.

"I can't believe this. Why . . . Why don't you want my seed?" His voice began to rise hysterically.

"Because I don't think I will be a good parent," I said with no feeling. I was tired of him screaming at me.

"Sasha, you are so damn selfish." He gave me a scorching look. "Everything always has to be about *you*. All I do for you, and you treat me this way. All this time, I've been trying to have a baby, and all along, you didn't even want one. This is unbelievable." He spoke through clenched teeth. "I'm out of here. I need some time to think." He stormed out of the bedroom and slammed the door behind him.

I sat on the bed and stared at the door after he was long gone. I was upset that he was hurt. But I was glad to get that off my chest. I wondered where our marriage stood after the way he left. He may not want to continue what we have, and to tell the truth, I don't think I did either.

11

Melody

Before Rayn and I made our trip to the mall, I had to do a photo shoot. My mind had been so distracted with Rodney's behind that I was starting to put my business on the back burner. I needed to get myself together. I shouldn't let no one come before my money. The doorbell rang, and when I answered it, there was a woman and her baby girl dressed in the same type of floral sundresses. They looked stunning.

"Um, how you doing? My name is Kim, and I'm here to get me and my daughter's pictures taken," the woman said as she chewed on a wade of gum. Her daughter swarmed on her hip.

"Hello and welcome to Rayn's Photography. I'm Melody, and I will be taking your photos today," I greeted them with a smile.

"Come on down. Your daughter is beautiful," I said as they followed me down the few stairs to my photo studio. I loved what I did. I had made photography my career after I graduated from college, and I have had my in-home studio for going on four years. I loved capturing family photos, but I also loved being the photographer at weddings. I get a few calls to take photos at special events around the city. I was in desperate need for a building, but for now, my business was in the lower level of my house.

My studio was set up real nice. I had my own backgrounds and props. I put a lot of money into my cameras and lighting equipment. I was professional about mine, and I wasn't going to be caught taking no janky pictures. I needed returning customers. I had bills to pay.

The mother-daughter session went well. Kim was kind of ghetto. I had to tell her to spit out her gum because she wouldn't stop chewing on it to take a photo. Her makeup was flawless, and her hair was tight. Her neatly braided micros were pulled on top of her head in a bun. Her three-month-old daughter's jet-black, curly, mini'fro was pulled back with an elastic headband with a small flower in the front that matched her dress. After the session was over, I asked her where she found out about my studio. She told me she saw my flyer at her man's house. I didn't ask her what his name was because I probably didn't know him. My cards were everywhere. I was grateful that she found out about me and that she supports black-owned businesses.

Rayn and I walked into Westfield Mall. My daughter loved going shopping. She was becoming a teen, and she loved nice things. She wasn't a girly girl. She didn't care too much about getting her hair done; she loved just wearing an Afro puff. I tried getting her some braids just to change up her style, but she told me that she didn't want to have weave in her hair because people would know it's not hers. I told her it would be paid for, so it would be hers. She didn't wear jewelry not even earrings, and she didn't keep her nails polished either. But she liked wearing sundresses and cute shoes.

I didn't like shopping at the mall because it seemed that all the clothes that were on the racks were made with floral designs and styles just for teens. But I had decided to come to look for bras. It was so hard for me to find a good fitted bra. I would shop at an expensive store like Victoria's Secrets and purchase one bra for thirty dollars or more. At the store, it would feel right when I tried it on in the fitting room, but once I got home and after wearing it a few times, my 34DDs would spill out of the top of the bra. It was hard to find size 34DDs, so I had to sometimes buy 36DDs. I wished I could just find a store where I could find a bra that fits.

"Mom, this dress is so cute. Can I get it?" Rayn said excited while holding a long, black and tan halter dress.

"That's cute. Yes, you can get it, but remember, your limit is forty-five dollars," I said. I searched the racks looking for a pair of jeans since this store didn't carry bras. After Rayn picked out a few things, I paid for them; then we headed to JCPenney's.

I found me a few bras, tried them on, and I prayed they'd work out after I washed them at home. Rayn started to look at more dresses. "Stay over here in this area. I'll be back, I'm going to the misses department to look at the Levi's."

"Kay, Ma," Rayn said as she combed through the racks.

As I looked through the shelf covered with neatly folded jeans, the scent of a nice masculine-smelling cologne lingered in my nose. I lifted my head up and saw Dominic.

"Hey, Melody, long time no see." Dominic smiled and walked over to me and gave me a hug.

"Hey, Dominic, it's been a long time no see," I smiled. I have not seen him in over five years. The last time I saw him, it was at the liquor store, and it was brief. He was buying liquor, and I was playing the lotto. We spoke, and he gave me his number, but I didn't call him because I was in a relationship.

"What you been up to?" he grinned. He always smiled, showing his pretty whites, and I loved seeing his smile.

"Nothing; just working. How about you?" I eyed him up and down just to see how he was looking. He was dressed in sweatpants, a tee shirt, and some dusty-looking sneakers. He was looking kind of dingy to be at the mall.

"I just got off work. I rode up here with my mom and sister to get me a pair of shoes."

I noticed the bag from Foot Locker in his right hand. Then he continued, "How is Rayn doing?"

"She's good; she's over there somewhere looking at some things." I pointed toward the Junior Department.

"I know she might not recognize me. How old is she now?" he grinned.

"She's twelve going on twenty-one." We both laughed. "But she's a good kid."

"You not married yet?" he asked, looking down at my ring hand.

"No." I smacked my lips and waved my hand in his face. "No ring."

"Well, let me get your number." He took his phone out of his pocket. I told him my number, and he saved it under his contacts.

"What are you doing tonight?" he asked, putting his phone back in his pocket.

"I might head out to Club Headliners with my cousins."

"Well, I might just see you out there then. We can catch up and get a few drinks."

"Okay," I said; then he rubbed the side of my face gently. I wanted to move back. I didn't know where his hands had been. As he walked away, I told him to tell his mom I said hi. And he nodded.

Dominic and I dated about eight years ago. He and Omar Epps could pass for twin brothers. He looked just like the young Omar when he played in *Love & Basketball*. They have the same eyes and lips, and they both had the same complexion. I would sometimes smile at him and call him Omar because it was crazy how much they looked alike. We dated for about two years. Our families were close. My mother used to date his uncle. He would joke and say that we could have been kissing cousins.

Dominic was cool when we were together, but we were young, and I would always suspect him of cheating. That was when Rayn's dad and I had broken up because he'd cheated on me. So when I got in the relationship with Dominic, it was just hard for me to trust him because I had been hurt before. I had never caught Dominic cheating on me, but he got tired of me accusing him of it.

I hoped he did pop up at the club tonight. That would make Rodney jealous. And I would be sure to throw it in his face. I wanted him to hurt like he hurt me. "Come on, Rayn, it's time to go to my favorite clothing store, Dots." Rayn followed behind me as I walked out of the mall. I was about to find something that would make all the boys turn their heads when I walked through the door, especially Rodney's. I grinned to myself.

12

Sasha

The buzz from my alarm clock woke me from the nightmare I was enduring while I slept. I jumped up. My silk nightgown was drenched in sweat, and so was my pillowcase. In the nightmares, I would be in a state of panic, locked in a dark room with hardly no room to breathe. I would be left for dead. Sometimes I would even be locked in a coffin, screaming and kicking, hoping that someone would hear my cry and save me from the distress I was in. But the night terror would always end the same. No one ever came to my rescue.

I looked at my husband's side of the bed. It was empty. He had not come home last night after the argument we had. I didn't really care. I was going to plan on having a peaceful day. I read a few chapters in the novel that I had gotten from the library. I also wrote a chapter in my erotic manuscript. I was excited because when I put my mind to it, I was able to develop my character and scene quickly and creatively. The short story I was working on would soon be a novel if I kept writing like I was. When I sat down and starting typing, I would get like 2,000 words in at a time. I didn't know I had it in me, but I was really thinking about getting my work published. I could see myself as the next Zane, being a top *Essence* bestselling author, having my own XXX late-night TV show on HBO, and even a hit movie from one of my novels on the big screen. Yes, I dreamt big. If she could do it, I could too.

I was getting tired of looking at the walls, so I made plans to step out to the club with Melody and Asia in a few hours. The club scene was becoming the only place we could have fun. The part of Ohio where we lived was so boring; the only fun things to do at night were bowling, movies, or clubs. So I chose the club scene. I needed to get lit.

I decided to give David a call just to say hello. We talked for about thirty minutes. I found out that he was the business manager at AT&T. He had no kids and didn't want any. Not that it mattered, but we had that in common. He told me he would stop by the club tonight to get another dance. I told him that didn't sound like a bad idea. I looked forward to seeing him. He made me feel sexy and free, feelings that my husband had never brought out of me.

I strolled through the doors of Club Headliners, and Asia and Melody frolicked behind me. Tonight was ladies' night. The men were gawking and drooling like hulks, and we were their prey. We walked over to the bar, and before we could order, some guy with a serious overbite crammed his body in front of me.

"Damn, damn, damn! Y'all sho' are the sexiest women up in here. Can I have the pleasure of buying your drinks?" He grinned as he looked at me but was talking to all three of us. He then waved two twenties in the air.

"You sure can," Asia piped in.

I didn't say a word. I was looking at his grill saying to myself he needed to take care of that. His teeth were such an eyesore I couldn't stomach talking to him. We told Mr. Overbite what we wanted to drink, he ordered; then we thanked him. I knew it wasn't going to be easy to get rid of him. But why was he all up in *my* face when Asia was the one who wanted him to buy the drinks?

He leaned his body close to mine and said, "Baby, I can't keep my eyes off you."

Dang, his teeth *and* breath were bad. I didn't say much to him because I wanted him out of my face. "I'm married."

"Well, is he up in here?" He licked his chapped lips.

"Yup," I lied. He needed to make a date with Listerine and Scope.

"Oh, well, okay. I don't want no problems. But next time you should warn a brotha before he buys you a drink," he said with a serious attitude and quickly stepped to Asia.

I laughed to myself and sipped on my drink. But then my eyes met up with a sexy guy that was watching me from across the bar. It was David. I smiled, and he walked himself over to me. Asia was still taking to Mr. Overbite, and I noticed that Melody was talking to one of her exes. I haven't seen Dominic in a while. He was still looking good. But I wondered if Rodney was watching her run game. He needed to see that someone else was interested in Melody because he just wasn't right, and she needed to stop being so weak and stupid over Rodney's dirty drawers. She needed to put her big-girl panties on and get rid of his behind. Enough is enough.

"You still sexier than ever," David said in my ear from behind me.

I smiled. "You lookin' pretty dapper yourself." He was causal, wearing a blue striped button-up shirt and jeans. He resembled Drake, but just dark skinned.

"I was watching you. I thought you had come here with your husband."

"Nope. Just me and my girls." I knew he was referring to Mr. Overbite.

"What are you drinking?" he asked looking into my glass.

"Cîroc, straight, no chaser," I smiled seductively.

"You bad. I like that." He licked his lips.

When I saw his tongue, it instantly made me hot as I thought about what that thang did to my body. He ordered my drink, we made small talk; then he asked me to dance. We dance through three songs, but on the last song, I couldn't take no more. I wanted him, and I couldn't hide my lustful desire for him. I could tell he felt the lust seeping through my pores.

As we danced, he brought his lips to my ear and tickled it with his tongue. "Are you ready to leave this joint?"

I nodded.

We were out of the club and in his car within minutes. This time, he drove, and I just sat back and listened to the jazz that he was playing. I waited to see where our destination would be. To no surprise, we ended up at the same spot. I shook my head and smiled to myself. I see he wasn't creative when it came to picking spontaneous spots, or maybe he just liked the park. But this time, we were not parked by the water. He pulled into the parking spot and turned the car off. He got out of the car and walked to the back of the car and opened the trunk. He then shut the trunk and walked over to my door and opened it. I got out to see that he was holding a large blanket.

I see he came prepared. "I ain't lying on no ground," I spat and looked in his eyes.

"Just come on," he replied as he took my hand.

We walked over to a wooded bench that was on a hill, and when I looked over the hill, I could see the Maumee River. He placed the blanket over the bench. He then took my hips and pulled me in close to him. He kissed me passionately, and while our tongues danced, he guided me over to the bench. He sat me down, sat next to me, and started kissing my neck. Then he pulled my dress past my shoulders, pulled my bra down, and my breasts popped out. He sucked on them vigorously, and my heart started to beat rapidly. I was excited and full of lust.

My breathing became intense as he continued to feast on my breasts, one at a time. Then he took my hands and placed them on my breasts as if he wanted me to massage them. I did. After that, he got on his knees and raised my short dress up high enough so he could get his tongue to my hot spot. He lifted my butt up with both of his hands and gripped it tightly as he nibbled on my womanhood like it was a cupcake.

I moaned. I whimpered. My toes curled as waves of euphoria filled my body. As my head lay back on the bench, I looked up at the stars that were sprinkled across the dark sky. "You are a beast," I belted out. I gyrated as I massaged my breasts, and he ate until he was full. As he was rising up from his knees, his eyes suddenly became huge like saucers as he looked over my shoulder. He scared the mess out of me, and I quickly turned to see what had him stunned. My heart dropped out of my chest.

"Jonathan," I gasped. I stopped breathing. But then I had to come to and put my boobs back in my bra and dress. I quickly stood to my feet after pulling my dress down.

"Oh, no, don't stop now. I was enjoying hearing my half-naked wife moan as some random dude devoured her like she was his for the taking." His voice was calm, but his face was filled with anger. I had never seen him that way.

"Jonathan, I—"

"Shut up, you little whore. So *this* is what you wanted when you said you wanted to be *free?*" he spat as he walked toward me. I thought he was about to hit me the way he glared at me, but David quickly walked in between us.

"Hold up, man," David piped in. I was shaken to my core.

"No, *you* hold up, bro. This is *my* wife." Jonathan shoved David so hard that he fell back a few feet.

Jonathan then charged at me and smacked me in my face.

"Ohhh," I cried out in pain. My hand shook as I grabbed my face where it stung. I looked at my hand. It was full of blood that dripped from my nose.

"You are a trifling bi—" Before Jonathan could get all of his words out, David punched him in the jaw, and he fell to the ground.

"Man, what you *ain't* gonna do is put yo' paws on no woman. You got paws, put them on *me*," he growled as he stood over Jonathan as he lay on the ground with a busted lip.

Oh God, what have I done?

13

Asia

As I was getting dressed for my date with Steve, I thought about how he had been such a good dad to all of my children. When he got out of jail almost a month ago, I thought he wasn't going to be able to find a job, and I was right. So he went out and started his own business. He was the CEO of Tight and Right Lawn Services. He started with one lawnmower, an old truck that his uncle gave to him, and family members' lawns. Now, he was cutting over twenty lawns a week with a riding mower that I helped him purchased.

"Babe, don't you worry. I'm going to pay you back all the money for the equipment. I'm so glad that you stood by my side, and I promise I'm going to make it up to you. I love you." That was what Steve told me after we picked up his used riding mower.

Steve and I meet at the club, and on the first night I met him, I ended up at his place. We had a nice evening, but he really wasn't my type. He wasn't that good in bed, so the morning after, I didn't call him. I wanted him to contact me. Yes, I flipped the script on his behind. Well, I guess that turned him on because he started blowing my phone up, and he couldn't get enough of me. But I didn't give him any attention until after I found out I was pregnant, and I knew it was his.

When I told him I was pregnant, he was ecstatic. But the thing was, he didn't have a legal job. I wasn't the type of chick that dealt with drug dealers. Well, let him tell it, he was a "pharmacist." I learned in the past to walk away from a man with that career choice. I was dealing with a dude awhile back, and my house was raided, and that scared me straight . . . to walk straight *past* drug dealers. Steve knew how I felt about what he did, and he told me that he had stopped. I believed him because he was discreet about what he did. But that was a lie, because he got pulled over by the cops, and they found drugs on him. That's when he went to prison. It was like an epidemic where I was from. It was sad, but it seemed like most of the men went to jail for selling drugs. All the females that I went to school with were dealing with a man going in and out of jail for a drug-related crime. The person that truly suffered was the child, because most of the men were fathers.

The ringing from my cell phone snapped me from my thoughts. "Hello."

"Hello, Asia, how are you?" my mom said.

"I'm good, Mom, how are you?" I asked as I tried to apply some foundation to my face.

"I'm a little stiff today from my arthritis because of the rain outside," she whined.

"Have you taken any pain pills?"

"Now, you know Charles don't like me taking all those pills. So I just take the little pain until it subsides."

My mom was the type to follow her husband. If he said jump, she would ask how high. Melody said that I was beginning to have some of her ways. She once told me that I catered to my men too much, and that I shouldn't spend my money on them. They should fork out *their* money on *me*. But I didn't mind helping my man out if he needed some money.

"Baby, how are the kids doing?" Mom asked.

"They running around the house like they crazy. Can't you hear them in the background?"

She laughed and said, "I miss my grandkids." My stepfather had stopped my mom from watching my kids because he said all I did was party, and if she kept on watching them when I went out, I would just keep having more for her to babysit. I loved my stepfather, but he could be a pain at times.

"How's Steve over there treating the kids?" she wanted to know.

"Mom, he's great with them. He has changed so much for the better, and I'm glad that I gave him another chance." I smiled from the warm feeling I had in my heart for Steve.

"Well, Asia, don't you go having more kids, okay?"

"I'm not, Mom."

"How is crazy ol' Melody doing? Is she still following after that no-good boy that she introduced to us at Thanksgiving dinner? Then a few months after that, she said that they were never a couple like she thought."

"Mom, they're not together anymore."

"Well, you said that last time, and they *were* back together. She is just too old for that. What's wrong with the girl? Why can't she find a good man and keep him?" she huffed.

My mom was always in everybody else's business. If there was gossip to be told, she was right in the middle. "Mom, it's just some no-good men out here and—"

"And Melody bumps into every single one of them," she said, cutting me off. "Any who, enough about Melody. What's going on with Sasha? You know I heard about her husband finding her in the arms of another man."

"Yes, Mom, I know you heard 'cause you don't miss a beat." I shook my head.

"Um, um, um, why would she go and do something so stupid? Arlene told me all that man wanted was a baby, and she didn't want to give him one. He makes good money too, so why go and mess that up?"

Arlene was Sasha's mother, and I don't know how *she* found out what happened between Sasha and her husband, because Sasha didn't even talk to her mother. They haven't been close since Sasha left for college. They really hadn't got along when we were growing up. I still don't know why they couldn't stand each other. "Mom, how did Aunt Arlene find out about Sasha?"

"Sasha's husband called Arlene and told her that her daughter was no good, and he was going to divorce her. But, baby, I know that she stole him from you anyways, so she got what she deserves for going after your leftovers. I bet she feels really stupid now."

Way back when we were in college, I had told my mom that Jonathan was my first crush. I didn't think she remembered that. She would have a kick out of it if I told her that the man Sasha cheated with was a man that I went out with, *and* the man that I told to go and holler at Sasha. But I thought I would keep that little bit of information to myself. "Well, Mom, I have to go. I have a date with Steve, and he's waiting on me."

"Bye, honey. I'll talk to you later. Kiss the kids for me."

"Okay, I will." I checked myself in the mirror one last time to make sure my makeup was on point. Then I went downstairs to let Steve know I was ready. I still had to figure out how I was going to break it off with Lance before he found out that I was back with my baby daddy. I enjoyed how Steve was treating me and the kids, but his sex sure didn't compare to Lance's. Was I ready to let that go?

Not at all.

14

Melody

That night, Dominic met me at the club. I didn't want to leave with him, but I did. I sat in my dark room and replayed what went down.

"I sure have missed the time we spent together back in the day." Dominic talked over the music.

I just smiled and looked around to see if Rodney was watching me talk to Dominic. I wanted him to see that I was a catch, and if he didn't hurry up and catch me, someone else would. But Rodney was nowhere to be found. He had been texting me every day since the day he told me that chick was living in his house. At first, I didn't respond; then after a few weeks had passed, I responded, and we talked on the phone. He just kept telling me he wasn't with no one, and I didn't have to worry about her. He loved me and wanted to see me soon. Of course, I gave in because I missed him, and I wanted him. My life was boring, and he excited me with our dates and sex life.

At the bar, I texted him and asked him why he wasn't in the bar. He told me he wasn't there because he would be gambling all night. So that meant I wasn't going to see him. I didn't want to go home alone, so Dominic and I rekindled an old flame.

I was driving myself insane. I knew I had no business taking Dominic home. Rayn had stayed the night with her friend. I was tipsy, and he was just a rebound because I couldn't be with Rodney and I didn't want to be alone. But the morning after, I felt like a slut, even though Dominic and I had relations in the past. I didn't want him to think that I was the type to be having one-night stands, because I wasn't. After we had great sex, he then told me that he stayed with his mama, and when we bumped into each other at the mall, that job he told me he had just come from was a one-time gig he was doing for his uncle. It was not a permanent job. I couldn't believe I slept with a man who lived with his mama and had no job! I was snapped out of my dark thoughts when I heard the phone ring. I looked at the caller ID and had no clue who it was. "Hello."

"Hey, sexy," a deep voice said on the other end.

"Um, who is this?"

"Tayvon."

Oh, I had forgotten that I gave him my number in the club. Tayvon and I dated many, many years ago. We didn't really date. I had a crush on him when I was in high school, and he was the only guy that I did have a one-night stand with. I didn't want to be with him because I was in a relationship with someone else, but I did want to see what he was working with. I was a mess back then, but know I am too old now to be playing games.

"Hey, Tayvon, how you doing?"

"I'm good. Are you busy?"

"No, just sitting around the house chilling."

"Have you eaten yet?" he asked.

"Nope."

"Well, why don't you come by? I cooked Sunday dinner."

"Oh, okay. That sounds good. Do you want me to bring anything?" I asked.

"Nope. Just bring yourself."

"Okay. I'm on my way." I didn't know what his intentions were, but I was bored, and all I wanted to do was get out of the house. So, all I would do was eat, chitchat, and come back home.

15

Sasha

A month had passed since Jonathan kicked me out after catching David and I making out on the park bench. Of course, Jonathan was furious, but he had no right smacking me in my face. He had never put his hands on me in the past. I was shocked when David came to my rescue. If he didn't, from the look in my husband's eyes, he would have killed me.

I didn't dare go to my house after that incident. I had David take me to the hotel. The next day, I called my husband to apologize, but he didn't want to hear it. He angrily told me to come and get my things, and he was in the process of filing for divorce. It hurt at first, but I had to really think about everything. I did love Jonathan, but I was not in love with him. The main reason why we got married was because I was pregnant. Maybe this breakup is what we needed.

I had been living in my new luxury one-bedroom apartment alone for a few weeks. The complex is very nice and quiet. My 800 square foot apartment is not as roomy as the 2,500 square foot home I shared with my husband, but it was just enough space for me. My apartment had an open floor plan with a fireplace, vaulted ceilings, and a skylight. My kitchen was small, but it had nice light-colored ceramic tiles on the floor and dark granite countertops. I had to shop for new furniture, and

I was very satisfied with the red leather love seat, chair, and sofa set for the living area, and a queen-size sleigh bed and dresser for my bedroom. My spacious walk-in closet was to die for.

I was sipping on Avion and feeling good. I rearranged the pillows on my bed so I could lie down when I heard my phone ring. I looked at the caller ID. It was Melody.

"Hey, Mel, what's up?" I said as I flopped down on my bed and lit a cigarette. I had stopped smoking for over two years, but with all the drama that was going on in my life, I needed the nicotine to calm me down.

"Girl, you sound real chipper from dealing with what you've been through."

"Girl, I'm good."

"Are you going to try to get Jonathan back? What you did was foul. But maybe he'll forgive you," she said matter-of-factly.

"Um, no, I'm not going to chase after him. I'll be just fine." I wasn't like her. I didn't need a man to defend me. She needed to worry about her problems and stay out of mine.

"So what's up with you and that guy? Isn't his name David?"

"Yup, and there is nothing up with us." I rolled my eyes. I knew Mel and I kicked it a lot, but I really didn't like telling her or Asia about my personal business, because they are known to go behind people's backs and gossip.

"Asia told me that she tried to warn you of their relationship."

"What relationship?" I froze in place. OMG, I never even asked David how he and Asia knew each other.

"David and Asia had sex while they were in college," she explained.

That dirty tramp. She knew she should have told me before I left the club with him. I didn't know I was mess-

ing around with *her* leftovers. That is so nasty. But I
didn't share my thoughts or feelings with Melody. "No,
I didn't know that, but what we had was nothing, and
we will not be seeing each other again." I knew Asia was
jealous of Jonathan and my relationship, but I didn't
think she would stoop that low. I couldn't wait to see
Asia because I had some choice words for her. "What do
you mean it wasn't nothing? Your husband is in the process of leaving you and—"

"How do you know that?" I cut her off.

"Mom said that your mother called her and told her
that Jonathan called her and told her everything," she
stuttered.

I knew the whole family would know what went down
because my husband had a big mouth. Every time we got
into it, he would call my mother, and my mother would
call everybody in her phone log *but* me. I haven't talked
to her since I went away to college, and that was how I
wanted it to stay. She had done some stuff to me that
I wouldn't wish on my worst enemy. She was the main
reason why I never wanted to have any children.

16

Asia

As I walked up to the Colonial-style home, I could see the couple sitting in their car. I waved at them letting them, know that I was the Realtor. I was dressed formal in my gray pencil skirt, a dark orange blouse, and my medium-sized pumps.

"Hello, I'm Asia Underwood, and I'll be showing you this house today," I said as I extended my hand to shake the wife's hand first, and then the husband's. They had called me and told me that they were a newlywed couple, and they were looking for a home that they can expand their family in.

"Hello, Ms. Underwood, this is my wife Kathy, and I'm Jim," the young redheaded man said with glee.

"Nice to meet you; please call me Asia," I smirked. "Follow me so I can show you this beautiful 2,350 square foot two-story home. The listing price is two hundred and fifty-three thousand. It's been on the market for about six months, so I can probably get that price lowered. The owners really want to get this place sold so they can move out of state."

"I love the landscape and the spacious porch," Kathy announced with excitement.

"Well, let's see the inside," I said after I opened the front door.

"Wow, I love the high ceilings! And, honey, look at the large bay window! It brings in so much sunlight to the living area." Kathy was on cloud nine.

"I love the brick fireplace," Jim pointed out.

"On the first floor, you have a formal dining room with dark wood floors and a carpeted living area. Let's check out the kitchen." I walked over to the kitchen, and they followed behind me.

"Wow, honey, this kitchen is huge. I like the forty-two-inch cabinets. The garnet countertops are gorgeous," Kathy said as she slid her hands across the countertop.

"It has the new stainless-steel appliances that you wanted," Jim piped in as he walked over to examine the refrigerator.

"Check out the ceramic tile floors," I piped in.

"They are gorgeous. One thing I don't like in here is the dark brown paint," Kathy replied.

"Oh, that's an easy fix. I can get a couple of gallons of paint and tackle that," Jim said.

"Oh, no, you won't. You can barely handle your tooth-brush. I'm not giving you a paintbrush," Kathy said, and they both burst out in laughter.

That was disgusting. I raised my brows at their enthusiasm and plastered on a smile. "Let's go upstairs to check out the bedrooms." After I showed them the upstairs, I took them out to see the huge fenced-in back-yard. The couple seemed to be very interested in the property, and they wanted to put their offer in. After I set a time and date for them to meet me at my office to sign the paperwork, I rushed over to meet Steve at Outback Steak House. He had made dinner reservations for us.

As Steve and I sat at the small table, he kept looking at me like he wanted to tell me something, but he was having trouble with spitting it out. Did he know that I was creeping behind his back with Lance? Was he trying to figure out how to tell me that he no longer wanted to be in a relationship with me? I really enjoyed the time we spent together over the past few months. His business was doing well, and I was selling a good number of homes. Everything was well. But I needed to tell Lance that we could no longer see each other. I wanted to be with Steve because my children would be devastated if I broke it off with him. Even though I was lustfully attracted to Lance, I needed to do what was best for my family.

"Baby, I got something to tell you," Steve stuttered, breaking me from my thoughts.

"Uh, what is it?" He was making me nervous. I saw the sweat beads on his temples.

"Do you love me?" he asked slowly.

Oh, no, he knows. "Yes, I love you." I swallowed the huge lump in my throat. *Lord, please don't tell me he followed me like Sasha's husband did and caught me in the act.* But why would he bring me to a restaurant to tell me *that?*

"You have really been by my side, and I really appreciate you. I appreciate you helping me with my business, and you have done a great job with raising the kids." He paused and took a sip of his water.

Here comes the . . . but, I thought to myself. I just sat silently and let him finish.

He reached his hand under the table as if he was getting something. He then stood to his feet in front of me. My eyebrows shot up in surprise . . . Was he about to—? Before I could get my thought out, he got down on bended knee and held out an open box. All I saw was a glistening two-carat diamond ring.

"Babe, I know this ring might not be as big as you may want, but I promise you I will get you something better when I can. I want to give you this token to show you that I love you and . . . Will you, um, marry me?" His face was soaked with perspiration.

"Oh my God, yes, yes! I *will* marry you," I cried out in joy. I got up to hug my man. The people seated at the tables around us cheered and congratulated us. After we let go of our embrace, I sat back down and examined my ring. Yes, it was small, but it was beautiful, and I loved it. I couldn't wait to tell Asia. But I really couldn't wait to tell Sasha the backstabber. I wanted to throw it in her face that *I* was getting married, and *she's* going through a divorce. She should've never married my first crush. But then my smile turned into a frown, and I had to catch myself because I didn't want Steve to see my expression. I looked at him. He was feasting on this thick, medium-well steak and creamy roasted potatoes. He wasn't paying me no mind. Now I *really* had to break it off with Lance. Something in my gut told me that he wasn't going to take our breakup lightly.

17

Melody

I had been really going through some things in the past week, and I couldn't believe the stuff that I was doing. I missed Rodney so badly, and I was so upset with him that I picked up random dudes to get over him. As I look in the mirror at myself, I'm ashamed of the reflection. What is this? Am I becoming a sex addict? But the only one I really wanted was Rodney. Why did I keep hopping in bed with other men that I'm not even in a relationship with? In the past, I would have never done that. All I want is love. Will I *ever* find love? My heart pumped spastically, and I had become weak in my knees as my tears clouded my vision. "All I want is to be loved," I cried out.

I went over Tayvon's house to eat, and I ended up having sex with him. I had come from being celibate for two years to having sex with three men within two weeks. I got in the shower and allowed the hot water to run down my back. I shook my head in pity at the woman I had become as I revisited the night I had with Tayvon.

"You really know how to cook. This roast is so tender. You are gonna have to tell me your recipe." I smiled at him as I sat on his love seat and ate the roast beef, macaroni and cheese, and cabbage that he cooked.

After we ate, we watched TV on his forty-two-inch flat screen. He sat on one love seat, and I sat on the other one across from him. His apartment was small and set up like a bachelor's pad. He had two black love seats and a small, rectangle cocktail table set in the middle of the floor. Under the TV was his stereo and his game set and what seemed like over one hundred video games that he must have collected.

"Are you full?" he asked and walked over to sit beside me.

"Yup," I answered. I was bored, and I was falling asleep. I should have gotten my butt up and went home. It was almost ten at night. He leaned over to me and grabbed my breast. He caught me off guard, but his aggressiveness turned me on. I sat still as he caressed both of my breasts in his hands before he lifted my shirt over my head. He then feasted on my breasts like they were his main course meal.

He slurped.

He licked.

He sucked.

He moaned and growled.

He held them tight and wiggled his face in between them. Then he started to bite on my nipple. "Ouch," I cried out. He was acting like a wild animal. At first, I was enjoying it. I moaned out from the pleasure that I felt. Then after about forty-five minutes or more, I was like . . . really . . . Is he ever going to stop? After he lifted his face off my breasts, his face and my chest were soaked with his saliva. He wiped his mouth off with his hand and looked in my eyes and said, "Damn, baby, your breasts are nice and sweet." I wanted to crack up laughing in his face, but I held my laughter in. It felt as if he sucked the black off of them. I was in pain by then. I guess he was a tittie man.

Then he pulled my pants down and placed them beside me on the couch. He propped my legs on top of his shoulders, and he went to town on my sweet spot just like he did on my breasts. I was in heaven. We both moaned as he gobbled me up. Another forty-five minutes went by before he got up and walked me to his bedroom. I checked my phone to see what time it was. It was after midnight. That fool had sucked me for two hours. Oh, I hoped his pipe game was tight because I was hot and ready to get my back blown out. We had sex once, about ten years ago. I couldn't remember if he was packing or not.

I lay my naked, moist body across his king-size bed that was covered with black satin sheets. It was pushed beside the wall, and there was no headboard.

"Damn, you are sexy," Tayvon panted as he gawked at my body. He put on his condom. It was dark in the room, so I couldn't see what he was working with. He crawled into bed and positioned himself over me as he probed with his manhood to find my entrance. Then he huffed and started to pump.

"It's not in yet," I said softly. My insides were waiting and wanting to take in what he had to give.

"Yes, it is." He panted like he was about to explode.

My body went limp from disappointment. You got to be kidding me. Then he pumped his last pump, exploded, and rolled over. I looked at him like he was disgusting. I wanted to say, "Is this a joke?" He was passed out. I got up and went to his bathroom to clean off and quickly put on my clothes.

"Are you leaving already?" he asked. He was still sprawled across the bed like he just worked a twelve-hour shift.

I sucked my teeth and rolled my eyes, "Yes, I have to work in the morning." I know he wasn't thinking of a round two.

He sat his naked butt on the bed and looked at me. "If you want it, you got it forever." He pointed to his heart with his finger and continued, "This ain't no one-night stand, baby. Let's cruise together."

I twisted my face up like he had farted and the smell had got to me. Then I thought for a second and said, "Are you trying to get me with Smokey Robinson lyrics?"

"What you talking about? Woman, that's D'Angelo's song," he said in his Gary Coleman voice.

I was speechless. Was he serious? I couldn't take him or the pinky finger between his legs. I just shook my head and walked out the door. He was a waste of my time. I so wished I was with Rodney.

The water to my shower turned cold and brought me back to reality. I was going to get dressed and see if Rodney would come by so we could talk. I was still angry at him, so I was avoiding him. I wanted him to miss me, so I didn't answer my phone or my texts. My body was growing feverish with desire just thinking about him. I was addicted to him. I needed to call him. I couldn't go another day without seeing his face. I searched my phone and dialed his number. My palms became sweaty, and my heart thumped against my chest as I waited on him to answer.

18

Sasha

I stood in my living room looking out of the bay window at the next-door neighbor's nappy-headed kids playing on my nicely manicured lawn. Then I walked at a fast pace out to the porch, yelled, and pointed my finger. "Get off my lawn; stay in your own yard." They looked at me as if I scared them. They got their behinds out of my yard with the quickness. Their mom had no control over them. They had their bikes and ball all over my grass. Just no respect at all for other people's property. I didn't want my yard looking like theirs.

Steve kept my yard tight. It looked as if my grass was fake, it was so perfect. The bushes that lined my house were trimmed neatly. My house had the best curb appeal. Now my neighbors were paying attention to my yard, and they were asking me how they could get in contact with my lawn guy. I was ecstatic to tell them that he was my fiancé.

Steve was not only keeping the outside of my house looking nice, but he also kept the inside clean. I think he was OCD because everything had to be cleaned and in order. I didn't mind it, though, as long as he didn't get on my nerves. He did have the nerve to tell me the other day to watch how I talked to my kids, that I shouldn't call them out of their names. I would've went off on him. But I counted to ten and calmly said, "These are *my* kids, and I will talk to them any way *I* please." He just walked out of the room. What I wanted to say was . . . Boy, don't come in *my* house trying to tell me how to interact with *my* kids. I was the one who gave birth to them, and I had been the only one taking care of them bastards their whole life.

I added the finishing touches to my makeup and headed out the door. I told Steve I was going to meet up with the girls, but I lied. I was going to meet up with Lance. It was time for me to tell him the truth. I no longer wanted to drag him along. I wouldn't want anyone to lead me on like I was doing him. For several weeks, I had been messing around with two men, and it was becoming real hectic for me to try to keep up with both of them. I was surprised that Steve hadn't noticed how I rushed to take a shower whenever I returned home from being with Lance. When I was being intimate with them, I prayed that I didn't slip and call the wrong name, and I hoped that they wouldn't be able to tell that I was cheating. I was really uncertain about which man I wanted to choose. But since Steve proposed to me, I had to get myself together and stop the little affair that I was having with Lance.

I walked into the small coffee shop and saw Lance looking all scrumptious, sitting at a table in the back. I had to control my sexual desire for him, because I was taken. I chose the coffee shop because I didn't want to lead him on by having him meet me a top-star restaurant.

"Hey, beautiful." He smiled and stood up and kissed me on my cheek. He always told me I was beautiful, and his words really helped me feel like I was.

"Hey, you." I sat down at the table across from him and gave him a settled look. I was about to break his heart, and I knew it.

"I haven't see you, and I've missed you over the past week. And when you called me, I wondered why you wanted to meet here, at a coffee shop, in the middle of spring. And you don't even drink coffee." He gave me a puzzled look.

"Well . . . I needed to tell you something."

He sat up in his chair. "What's wrong?"

On the way here, I thought about how I was going to break the news to him. As I looked into his sad puppy dog eyes, I wanted to lie but decided that I needed to give it to him straight, no chaser. I inhaled and said, "Lance, I'm sorry, but we can't see each other after today." Then I let out a deep breath.

"What?" His face darkened with pain. His expression scared me. I went mute.

"Did you just dump me?" he growled and gave me an evil glare.

"I just think it's time for us to go our separate ways," I stuttered.

"Why? Is there someone else?" His lips curled with disgust.

No, is what I wanted to say, because it looked like if I said yes, he would've hauled off and smacked me. "My baby daddy just got out of jail, and he wants to try to work it out." I looked in his fiery eyes, then threw in, "For the kids."

"You lying bi—" The waiter walked up to our table and stopped Lance in the middle of his sentence.

"Can I get you two anything?"

"Yea, you can get her a toe tag 'cause she gonna need it." Lance was talking to the waiter, but he glared at me.

Chills ran up my spine. I swallowed dryly and said, "We don't need anything right now." I gave the waiter a reassuring look so he would know everything was fine. But he was staring at Lance's expression. *Was* everything going to be fine? The waiter slowly walked away.

"What is that on your finger?" He was sharp with his words.

Dang. I forgot to take the ring off. "Oh, this thing . . . It's a friendship ring." I was lying through my teeth, and when I looked up at Lance, I could tell that he knew I was lying.

"You must think I'm a damn fool. So you been playing with me all this time?" he bellowed ferociously.

"No, Lance, I haven't been playing you." My eyes widened incredulously. I was trying to hide the guilt from my face, but I don't think I was doing a good job.

"Yes, you have. You been sexing me *and* that dude?" He stretched his arm across the table and grabbed my arm tightly.

I froze for a second. I couldn't believe what was happening. Then my mind came back to reality. "Let me go," I shouted through clenched teeth. I snatched my arm away from his hold, and his glass of ice water crashed to the floor.

The waiter walked over to intervene. "I'm sorry, but I'm going to have to ask you two to leave the premises immediately." He tried to be professional, but I could see fear in his eyes.

He put his hands on me, and that was enough for me to get up and walk out. As I made it to my car, Lance followed me. "You are dirty. I trusted your conniving behind. I told you that I had just gotten over a bad relationship, and you gonna play me like they did. I knew I shouldn't have trusted a whore like you. She was black, so I thought if I tried to be with someone out of my race, I would be better off. But ain't none of y'all chicks loyal." He spat at me. I could feel his breath and the saliva that sprayed in my face.

I begin to shake from fear as he threw daggers at me with his words. "I told you I was hurt before, and you came here to tell me you got someone else, and you wearing this diamond on your finger, in *my* face." He grabbed my finger as if he wanted to break it off.

"I'm sorry, but I got to go. You need to calm down." That was enough for me. I snatched my hand from him and hurried up, got in my car, closed the door, and locked it.

He tried to open the door. "You sorry! You sure are sorry, you little whore. You thought you was going to have a perfect little affair with me. This ain't no perfect affair. This ain't over. Trick, you hear me? You're gonna pay," he yelled as he kicked my truck and punched the window. I sped out to get away from his crazy behind.

It was getting dark outside as I drove home. I thought about how Lance had never acted like that in the past. I felt bad that I hurt him. Then I remembered that he did tell me that his last relationship ended on bad terms because the chick cheated on him and did him dirty. He told me that he was betrayed to the fullest and that he was really in love with her. He thought that he wouldn't be able to trust any other woman ever again. But I didn't plan to cheat on him, Steve just popped back into my life, and I was woman enough to break it off with Lance before it went too much further. Lance and I weren't together that long. I didn't think he was that attached to me. I didn't think he would go off on me like he did. I cared for him, but it wasn't that serious.

While I was deep in thought, I felt a hard thump at my bumper, like someone had rear-ended me. I slowed down my car and looked out the rearview mirror. I was in shock. It was Lance in his blue Dodge pickup truck. As my car came to a stop, he ran into the back of my SUV again!

"What the hell is wrong with you?" I shouted at the top of my lungs. I knew he couldn't hear me because my windows were up. He slammed into my back end *again*. I looked around. No one was on the street. I had to get away from him because he wasn't going to stop. So I put the pedal to the metal and drove. I was scared out of my mind. I griped the steering wheel tightly, and my palms sweat uncontrollably while my heart pumped spastically.

Then another crash to my backside. My head jerked forward, and I gasped for breath. I could hear the damage he was causing to my vehicle. The glass shattered in the back. I was going eighty miles per hour, and I almost lost control of my car. He was trying to kill me. My hands trembled as I tried to get my phone to call the police, to call someone to get this maniac off of my bumper. Tears filled my eyes. I was scared for my life. "Lord, please help me," I cried out. I then tried turning right. As I turned the corner, he came out from the back and slammed his truck into my passenger's door. I screamed out of fear and slammed on the brakes. My SUV flipped, I don't know how many times. I lost count after the second flip. Suddenly, everything went black.

19

Melody

I sat on the couch and watched all the drama that was going down on *Love & Hip Hop Atlanta,* my favorite reality show. These chicks had me cracking up. MiMi finally told the truth about her sex tape. I wanted to get my hands on that tape just to be nosy. She should be ashamed of herself. I don't care how much money I would get paid, I would never let no man videotape what goes down between us behind closed doors. MiMi had a daughter that one day will see that tape.

The doorbell snapped me from my thoughts. I flicked the TV off and got up, pulled the T-shirt that I was wearing down to cover my black lace boy shorts, and walked over to the door. I had butterflies in my stomach because I knew who was on the other side of the door.

"Hey, babe," Rodney said after he saw my face. I had invited him over so I could get some things off my chest.

"Hey," was all I could say as I looked into his dreamy eyes. He gave me that crooked smile that made me weak in the knees. But I had to remind myself what he was here for. We needed to talk. No, that's not all we did was have sex. We talked about everything. We talked about our goals and our future. We barely argued about anything. The only thing I didn't understand was why he was not ready to commit to our relationship.

He walked in and let the door slam behind him and planted a wet kiss on my cheek. "Umm, you smell good." He then tried to see what was under the long T-shirt I was wearing. I smacked his hand and switched over to the couch and flopped down. "I missed you, babe. I haven't seen you in weeks, and I have been so miserable without you. I'm sorry if I hurt you. Can we please just make up?" He walked over and sat next to me. At that very moment, he reminded me of Leon when he played *Waiting to Exhale*.

"What are you sorry for, Rodney?" I spat.

"Umm, I'm sorry that you think I'm trying to hurt you. I love you, and I need you in my life, and I would never intentionally hurt you. I don't want to argue." He gazed at me candidly.

"I don't want to argue either. All I want is to be the only woman you need in your life." I tried to be strong and swallow back the tears, but I couldn't stop them. He was my heart, and I was so emotional when it came to him.

"Please don't cry, baby." He leaned in close to hug me.

"I don't want your pity," I said and pushed him back. "I want you to love me like I love you," I said as I banged on his chest with both of my fists.

Rodney took his arms and wrapped them around my body, and my fists were still against his chest. "Melody, I love you, and only you. Let me make it up to you." He whispered his words in my ear.

I wanted to fight him. I wanted to cuss him out. I wanted to ask him why he was over there playing house with that ghetto bimbo if he loved me. But those words he just told me comforted me, and I was locked in his love trance. He put his hand under my shirt and slipped his finger inside my panties. I moaned, and my body went numb. I couldn't move a muscle. He handled me, and he handled me well.

As he tongued me down, between breaths, he said, "Babe, I swear, you are the only one I want."

I moaned.

"Babe, you taste so good."

My toes curled.

"Melody, I love you."

I cried out his name. I released, and he took all my sweetness in.

He got up off of his knees and crawled on top of me and filled me with the best of him, and my womb clenched him snugly.

"Oh my Gawd," I cried out.

"Damn, baby, you feel so good." He moaned as he stroked me slowly and gently.

I closed my eyes as I reached my height of ecstasy. And then, I felt his liquid shoot deep inside of me. We were so hungry for each other that he didn't put a condom on.

We lay in each other's arms and enjoyed each other's presence. Then I blurted out. "You know you came in me, right?" I had never slipped up like that before. I always used protection.

"Yeah, I'm sorry. You was feeling so good." He kissed me on the forehead. "But don't worry. I'll give you the money for that morning-after pill."

Then my phone rang, and my heart pumped fast in my chest. Who was calling me in the middle of the night? Oh Gawd, I hope it wasn't Dominic . . . Or Tayvon. I was going to act like I didn't hear it, but then, "Ain't you going to answer your phone? Who is it? Your boyfriend?" Rodney harshly said.

I smacked my lips. "No." I slowly went for my phone, hoping the ringing would stop. I looked at the number. It was unfamiliar.

"Hello," I said with an attitude.

"Hello, is this Melody Dickson?" a lady on the other end said.

I cleared my throat. "Yes, who is this?"

"My name is Linda, and I'm a nurse at Mercy Hospital. Your name was in Asia Underwood's medical file as her emergency contact and—"

I cut her off. "Asia's in the hospital? Is she okay?" I cried out in panic. My temple throbbed as I thought the worst.

"Yes, she is sedated right now. I cannot tell you—"

I cut her off again, "I'm on my way! Tell her I'm on my way." I got out of bed and without saying anything to Rodney, said, "I'll drive." My chest was heavy. I hoped my cousin was going to be all right.

20

Sasha

I had to get a hold of my husband, because I wanted to know why in the world he was calling my mother, a person that I had no ties with in years, and telling her our business.

As I sat on my love set and sipped on a cup of hot green tea, I thought about how Asia looked as she lay in that hospital bed. Melody called me in the middle of the night and told me that she was in a bad car accident, so I went to the hospital to see how bad it was. I was still mad about how she played me by not telling me that she was with David first. But I had to go and check on her, and I would leave soon after. Asia had a collapsed lung, a broken ankle, and her face was banged up pretty badly. The doctor said when the rescue squad brought her in, the police report said that her vehicle had flipped over, and it was totaled. There were no witnesses, so they don't know what caused the accident.

When we arrived, she was knocked out from the pain medication. Melody and I stayed there with her for a while, and then her fiancé told us that he would spend the night with her. Melody had informed him that we would stop by the next morning and check on her. She should let me out, because I had no plans on returning.

Jonathan told me he would be over an hour ago and still hadn't made it. I was beginning to think that he stood me up. Then I heard my bell ring. I buzzed him in.

When I opened the door, he gave me a look that said he really didn't want to be bothered. "What did you call me over here for?"

"Hello, come in," I said ignoring his attitude, as I looked him up and down. He looked nice, wearing a casual button-up shirt and some black jeans that didn't sag but fit him just right. He walked in and looked around my apartment but didn't say a word.

"Have a seat." I extended my arm, pointing at the couch.

"What am I here for?" he asked nonchalantly. When I called him, all I said was that it was important that we talk.

"Asia is in the hospital."

His eyes got wide. "Is she okay?" he said in a concerned voice.

"She was sedated when I saw her. She was in a car accident and broke a few bones, but she should make a full recovery," I said not feeling like going into full details.

"Wow. Well, I hope she has a speedy recovery." Jonathan knew how Asia felt about him. I had told him that she looked at him as her teenage crush. He laughed it off. He said the only reason he kissed her was because it was a dare his buddies made him do. He said that Asia was not his type because he didn't date white girls. She was easy, and she was sloppy built. He made it clear that he wasn't a racist. He just didn't date outside his race.

"But that's not what I asked you to come here for," I said getting back to our conversation.

"What is it? I ain't got all day." He gave me a cold look.

"Why did you call my mother and tell her what was going on with us?"

"Oh, so, is this what you called me over here for? You could've asked me that over the phone." He sat up straight as if he was ready to get up.

"Hold up. I just want to know why you called her. You know that her and I don't talk and haven't talked since I left home after high school," I said, my voice a higher octave.

"You know what? I always said to myself how a woman could respect her husband when she don't ever talk to her mother, and that's disrespect to the fullest power."

"Really!" I said at a loss for words.

"Yes, really. I always wanted to know why you and your mother never talked. Why your mother didn't even come to our reception after we were married. Or why . . ." he paused, and then swallowed the lump in his throat, "she didn't come around when we lost our firstborn."

Was he *really* still feeling some type of way about the miscarriage? He needed to get over it. I then thought to myself, *Maybe I needed to get over a few things in my past also.*

"Tell me, Sasha, why aren't you and your mother close? What has she done to you that makes you not want her to be a part of your life? When I talked to her, she seems like a nice lady," he said, looking at me as if he was looking into my soul for an answer.

"She seems nice because she's crazy. She can be nice one day and mean the next. She abused me, and she never wanted me from the beginning," I shouted. All the pain from my childhood rushed me like a derailed train going at high speed.

"Tell me what happened," my husband said in a concerned voice. He had asked me plenty of times in the past, but I didn't feel it was important for him to know the pain that I had endured as a child. The events of my past flooded my memory as if it were just yesterday.

***

I had come in the house from school, and my mom was sitting on the couch watching TV. I never knew what day she was having until she would have a "fit," that's what I called them. Every time she would abuse me or go crazy for no reason, I would say she was having a fit.

"Hi, Mom," I said as I passed her to go to the kitchen to get a snack.

"Where have you been?" she screeched.

I gave her a puzzled look. "I was at school, Mom."

"I've been looking all over for you. I thought they took you." She was pacing the floor in a cold sweat. I knew then that she was about to have a fit.

"Mom, please don't work yourself up . . . I'm fine. I was at school. Now, I'm going upstairs to do my homework," I said trying to calm her down.

"Don't tell me not to work myself up." She growled like a wild animal. Then she yanked my arm, and my school books fell from my hands. "Come on, you got to hide. I don't want them to get you."

She pulled me and guided me to the closet. I kicked and screamed. "Mom, please don't do this." I tried every time to break free because I knew what was about to happen.

She pushed me into the small coat closet that was right by the front door. And then she locked the door. "Be quiet. You'll be safe from them here. Don't be scared. I'll protect you," she would tell me in a calm voice.

I would bang on the door and cried for her to unlock the door. Most of the time after I became exhausted from screaming and banging on the door, I would hear her laughing and talking to the TV, which was near the closet that I was locked in. Sometimes she would lock me in her bedroom closet and leave the house and come back and tell me that she didn't want me to go out in public with her because she was afraid that they would take me from her. I would ask her who "they" were. She would always say "the bad people" or "the devil."

She would leave me locked up for hours. Sometimes she would lock me up with food, and sometimes she would lock me behind closed doors for the whole day. No one in my family knew what was going on because I was scared that I would be put in a foster home with strangers if I told them. So I just kept it a secret.

One night she was so angry because she thought that the bad people were in me, in my soul. She tried to shake them out of me. She shook. I screamed and cried. She shook me harder until we both heard a cracking sound. She had fractured my arm from pulling and yanking on it. But she didn't take me to the hospital because she said that the bad people will take me from her. So she made me suffer and sleep with a fractured arm. The next morning she did take me to the doctor and told them I fell out of a bunk bed that we didn't own.

"Wow, Sasha, that's terrible. That's why you be having all those terrible nightmares?"

I nodded my head. Tears trickled down my face. I didn't realized how much hurt I still had inside from that. But after I released that to someone for the first time, it felt like a huge weight was lifted from me.

"You shouldn't have been afraid to tell me that. That's deep. Has she ever gotten any help to see why she did that to you?"

"She did it because she didn't love me. She didn't want a child; she didn't want me. She was selfish, and she locked me up in those closets because she couldn't stand to look at me, and she didn't want to be bothered." I was outraged. My blood boiled, and my head felt like I had been hit by a semitruck. I needed a drink. I walked over to my kitchen, poured a shot of Avion in a glass, and chugged it down.

"No, to me, it seemed to me like she was going through something. Or maybe she had a disorder. Maybe she's bipolar or schizophrenic."

"No, the broad just didn't like me," I said getting frustrated. He was acting like he was some type of doctor. "That woman put me through hell for almost my whole childhood. I would try to stay at Asia and Melody's house as much as I could because I didn't want to be home." I swallowed hard, wiped the tears from my face, then continued. "Other times, my mother was a good person, and we shared some good memories in my early years of life. But it seemed like every year as I got older, she got worse. And now, she doesn't bother to call me, and I don't call her," I confessed.

"I'm telling you, it seems like she has some type of disorder. You said she talked to herself, and she always thought someone was out to get you." He folded his hands as if he was going to figure out a cure for why my mom did what she did. He was really irritating me. He annoyed me because he thought he knew everything. I just snapped.

"Whatever, man. You always think you can solve the problem. All this time you wanted a baby, I knew from the get-go that I didn't want a baby. I didn't want to be like my mom. I didn't want to repeat the cycle. So I knew God saved me by making me go through that miscarriage," I spat. Jonathan's eyes got wide. But I continued. I was on a roll, and no one was going to stop me from getting all my truth out.

"Jonathan, I never, *ever* wanted to get pregnant. Every night when you were trying so hard to put a baby in me, I already knew it wasn't happening. I refused to be like my mother. So right after I lost the baby, I went to my doctor and had him put me on birth control." There. I said it.

It was out. I looked at my husband's face, and his face flushed with anger. He gasped for breath. It looked as if he was going to pass out.

He stood to his feet and towered over me as I sat. "You little lying, conniving skank. All this time you have been on birth control. I should strangle the life out of you. But you know what? You are not even worth it. I was beginning to feel sorry for you for what your mother did to you. But you deserved all the torture she put you through. Y'all both need help. I can't believe I married someone like you." His voice was as cold as death. "I'm out of here before you make me do something crazy. You dirty. You real dirty." He had his fist balled up to his side. I looked at his dark expression on his face and sat frozen because I was scared that if I flinched just a little, he would knock all the teeth out of my mouth. He walked over to the door and let himself out. I didn't turn to see if he was gone. I sat there long after he left staring at a spot on the wall. I had finally got that off my chest, but it seemed as if my heart had just broken into a million tiny pieces and fallen to the floor. I had no energy to pick them up and mend my heart. I knew that I had lost my husband now, and he wasn't coming back.

21

Melody

Two months later . . .

"Rayn, you can cut up the sweet potatoes while I clean and season the cabbage." I always took time out every week so that my daughter and I could talk and prepare dinner together. We needed that one-on-one time together. She was growing up so fast, and I didn't want that time to slip away without us cherishing it.

"Okay," she said as she got out the potato peeler and the cutting board. We were preparing fried chicken, cabbage, corn on the cob, sweet potatoes, and corn bread.

As I was placing the battered chicken into the sizzling oil, Rayn said, "Mom, I really like Rodney, because he always take us to nice restaurants." She grinned.

"Yes, Rodney is a cool dude." I gave her a half smile. I always schooled my daughter on how men could be. I wished I could protect her from men that would try to break her heart, but I knew I couldn't. And one day, I knew she was going to come to me with a broken heart, and I would always be there to talk her through it.

"Baby, just because a man takes you to nice restaurants, that don't mean they have your best interest at heart. Sometimes, they just like to spend money on you and treat you real good so they can get what they want." I had talked to her about sex and waiting until she was married plenty of times, and I was going to keep talking to her about it.

"So, are you saying that Rodney is *not* a nice guy?" She looked so innocent. If she only knew what he was putting me through. I would kill a dude if I knew he was treating her like Rodney treated me. Why couldn't I defend myself in my own situation like I would if it was my daughter's problem?

"Rayn, Rodney and I have been knowing each other for a long time, and we are working through our issues. Every couple has their ups and downs. But I don't want you to settle. When the time is right for you and God sends you your mate, don't you let him get away with any nonsense. You stand firm and tell him you ain't the one, and you are only going to expect the best. You hear me?"

"Yes, Mama."

Now if I only could stand firm in my relationship. It was easy to talk the talk but hard to walk the walk.

"Girl, you did your thang with making the corn bread and the sweet potatoes. But your Kool-Aid was a little sour," I said, and we both laughed. We finished up our delicious dinner and then headed to bed because Rayn had a game early in the morning.

"You played a great game today," I said as we headed to the car.

"Thanks, Mom. I'm glad we won 'cause I was tired of losing," she belted out with joy. Rayn had been playing basketball for her school for the past four years. She was pretty good at it. I tried to keep her busy and athletic. She was also a cheerleader for her school's football team.

"Mom, can I go over Jasmine's house? Her mom wanted to make us tacos, our favorite, for winning the game."

"Yes, but you should go home and change your clothes first."

"Mom, I'll be all right. No one else is changing their clothes. I don't stink," she said, pulling her jersey to her nose and sniffing it.

I smiled. "Okay, I'll drop you off and can run some errands, and then come back to get you."

"Cool," she cheered.

After I dropped Rayn off, I decided to go over to Rodney's house unannounced. We had just made love the night before. He seemed to really be in to me, and I knew that he would be ready to give me that title of being his woman, especially after I tell him the good news that I had been holding on to.

I drove up to Rodney's house—and my heart dropped when I saw that white Dodge Charger parked in his drive-way. It was time to meet his "roommate," since he said I had nothing to worry about. I parked my car in front of his house and walked to the porch and rang the doorbell. A high yellow chick with pimples that covered her entire face answered the door. I wanted to give her the number to Proactive. She rocked a mini-Afro that was screaming for a wash and deep condition treatment. She looked ratchet and tore down.

"Can I help you?" she said, smacking on a wad of bubble gum as she looked out of the screen window in the door that had security bars attached to it. She looked familiar, but I couldn't remember from where.

"Yeah, is Rodney here?" I asked with an attitude.

"Yeah, he here, but who are you? I've seen you before. Do I know you?" She twisted up her face like something stank.

"I'm his woman, and, no, you don't know me, but you about to know who I am," I said with dignity.

"Rodney, there's some chick out here claiming she's yo' woman." She shifted her body and called out to Rodney.

I heard him yell out, "What?"

When she turned, I saw a small baby in her arms. I then knew who they were. That was the chick named Kim that was at my house. I did a photo shoot for her. She told me that she found my card at "her man's" house. Damn! Makeup made her look like a totally different person. No, he didn't have her and her baby living in his house. This couldn't be happening. That better not be his baby. Before Rodney made it to the front of the house, the chick opened the door and told me to come in.

"I'm Kim, and this is Stink Stink, Rodney's and my three-month-old daughter." She made sure she told me all the details. I wanted to cry, but I wasn't going to let her see me go out like that. When Rodney saw my face in his home, the home where we had share many sleepless nights in, his eyes were as wide as saucers. He looked like he had just seen a ghost, with shock written all over his face. I just waited to see what he was going to say to get himself out of this one.

When I came in, the girl finally realized who I was. "Oh, snaps, you took me and my baby's picture. You that photographer. Rodney had your cards all on his dresser. What, Rodney, you promotin' this trick's business?" She patted her weave with her hand to stop the itch. She then looked at Rodney sideways once he made it up to the door.

"Mel, what are you doing here?" He stammered over his words, ignoring everything that Kim had said.

But Kim continued her rant. "Oh, don't start stuttering now. Boy, you are so full of it, you didn't tell this woman that you had a newborn baby? You didn't tell her that we lived together?" She snapped at him with one hand on her hip and the baby on the other hip.

"Kim, go in the other room so I can talk to her," Rodney boomed. Kim looked at him as if she was going to say *hell, no, I ain't going nowhere.* But then she turned and stomped out of the room like a pouty toddler. I was speechless. The words that wanted to come out were stuck in my throat.

"This is not what it looks like." He leaned in and talked low. "She is staying here because she got put out, and I didn't want her to be living on the street with the baby. I ain't even sure if that's my baby. We're getting the blood test soon. But you and I wasn't ever kickin' it when she got pregnant." He talked fast, as if he was in a race to finish what he had to say first.

My stomach was in knots as I gave him a frigid stare. I wanted to shank him right where he stood.

"You are a liar. You should have told me that from the get-go. But, no, you lied and told me your pipes was broke and you got a chick and a baby staying here." I grinded out the words between clenched teeth. My blood was boiling.

"I'm sorry," he said, then turned to see if his supposedly baby mama could hear him.

"You are a good-for-nothing dirty dog, and you are going to pay for what you have put me through," I cried out. My hands shook as I reached into my purse and grabbed the stun gun that he bought me to use to protect myself. His eyes widened at the object that was in my hand, and before he could say a word, I zapped his behind right in the stomach. I tried to aim for his chest, but my hands weren't stable enough. He moaned and did a little jig. I turned and speed-walked to my car before I saw him hit the floor. I heard his chick call out his name in a panic. I hoped he was dead after how he treated me. I wanted his heart to feel the pain that I had been feeling from his disloyalty. I hopped in my car and put the pedal to the metal and sped off without looking back.

22

Asia

I got myself into this situation, and I had no clue of how I was going to get out of it. Lance had really tried to kill me. He left me on the road to die. The police told me that there were no witnesses that saw the accident. I'm glad he didn't know where I lived because he'd probably try to stalk me. Was he going to continue to harass me by calling my phone? I had to tell Steve about everything.

I lay in my bed in deep thought. My ankle still ached after the car accident I was in almost two months ago. I spent four days in the hospital, one of my lungs had collapsed, and my ribs were cracked. I broke my ankle in two different spots. I remember screaming and yelling at the doctor. They had to cut me open on the side of my breast and put a tube in me to keep fluid from going into my lungs. I kept telling them to put me to sleep, but they wouldn't. When they were done, I was so exhausted from trying to fight the doctors off of me. Steve told me that the doctors said that I passed out after I saw all my blood and guts all over the floor.

My ankle was still swollen, and I had to be pushed around in a wheelchair when I first got out of the hospital because my lungs still had to heal, and I couldn't put any weight on my ankle. I would have a rod and screw in my ankle for the rest of my life. I had to go to therapy every week for my ankle. Melody came to visit me every day.

She told me that Sasha came to visit me the first night; I didn't see her. They told me I was asleep. Melody told me a few days before I had the accident that Sasha was mad at me for not telling her I slept with David. She would get over it just like I had to get over her marrying my first crush. She was just salty because from what I heard from my aunts, Jonathan is about to divorce her. God don't like ugly.

"Hey, babe, how are you feeling?" Steve asked, taking me from my thoughts. He handed me a glass of orange juice and my pain pill that I was supposed to take when needed. He could tell that I was in pain because I hated lying in bed during the day.

"I would be okay if my ankle would stop throbbing." I let out a long sigh.

"I know, babe, I can't wait till you feel better. I know you're miserable." Steve had been by my side from day one. He wanted to cancel all of his lawn appointments to be home with me. But I told him that he didn't have to put his business on hold. My son Joey could keep an eye on me.

"Do you need anything else? I'm about to go downstairs and cook dinner," he said as he fluffed my pillows for me.

"Okay, I'm good." I gave him a welcoming smile. He was amazing.

As I sat back and flipped through the channels on the TV, I thought back when my kids first came to see me at the hospital. Joey came up to me, and his face was red. Tears streamed from his eyes.

"Aw, honey, I'll be okay. Stop crying," I told him, and even though I was in excruciating pain, I motioned for him to come closer to give me a hug.

He sobbed on my chest. "Mom, was you trying to kill yourself? I'm sorry. I'll be a better son. I'll try not to break your dishes when I wash them. I promise I'll be more careful."

"Honey, why would you say that? Why do you think I would try to kill myself?" I asked as I lifted his chin so I could look him in his eyes. Steve listened as he held my two youngest kids back so that Joey and I could talk.

"You always say that we stress you out and that you can't stand us. You always scream at us and call us names. I thought . . ." He paused and swallowed the lump in his throat. "I thought you would rather be in heaven than to be here with us."

My heart dropped, I was so sad that my son thought that. Oh my God, what was I doing to my kids? "Joey, no, I didn't try to kill myself. I am so sorry that I have been so mean to you and your sisters. I love you, you hear me?"

He nodded his head and wiped the tears from his cheeks.

"You are a good boy. I need to work on me so I can be a better mother, okay?" I held back the tears that were fighting to come out. I looked at Steve, and he gave me a look that said, "I told you that you needed to stop being mean to these kids."

After my talk with Joey, Angel and Alexa came over, and with help from Steve, I was able to give them a kiss. I couldn't wait to get out of the hospital. I had work to do. I had to work on showing my kids that I loved them.

My phone rang and broke me from my thoughts. I fumbled around the bedspread trying to find my cell phone. I looked at the caller ID. It was Melody.

"Hey, girl." My voice was tired.

"Hello, Asia, I was just checking on you. How are you feeling?" She sounded as if she had run a race. She was out of breath.

"I'm feeling okay, but what's goin' on with you? You sound all out of breath."

"Girl, I'll be all right. My life is complicated, but I don't want to talk about it," she said in a rush. I knew it was because of Rodney, but I wasn't going to pry her for information. When she was ready to talk, she would.

"I'll talk to you later. I have to go. Call me if you need anything."

"Okay, thanks for checking on me," I said before I hung up the phone.

As soon as I put the phone down, it rang again. I figure it was Melody and she was ready to talk about her situation now. I didn't bother to look at the caller ID this time. "Hey, girl, are you ready to talk?" I pushed my words out like I was ready to be her listening ear.

"Damn, you still alive?" the person on the other end said coldly.

I cringed at the voice. It was Lance. The call was unexpected. The harshness from his words were unexpected. I started to tremble. I gaped in stunned silence.

"If you dare tell anyone that it was me . . . I will come after you, your kids, and your little jailbird husband-to-be. You tried to keep your home a secret from me, telling me you didn't bring men around your family. Well, I got news for you, you nasty slut. I know where you lay your head at night." He then read off my address. My heart dropped in my lap.

"Say one word and I will blow up yo' house with all y'all in it. I'm not through with you yet." He left out a devious laugh. Then I heard the dial tone buzzing in my ear.

It took me awhile to catch my breath from the blow that went straight to my chest. I sat there with the phone still up to my ear and sobbed uncontrollably.

23

Melody

I didn't want to tell Sasha what happened, and I knew that Asia was still recovering from her accident, so after I made it home, I called to check on her. After that, I called my mother. I knew she was tired of hearing me go through it with Rodney, and I knew she was going to tell me to leave his behind alone. But I needed someone to talk to, so I dialed her number.

"Hello," my mom cheerfully greeted me like she had no care in the world. She stayed in Michigan, which was about an hour away from Rayn and me. I would visit her at least once a month.

"Hi, Mom."

"Oh, Lord, Mel, I know something is wrong. I can hear it in your voice. Please tell me Rayn is okay." She was concerned.

"Yes, Mom, Rayn is just fine," I reassured her.

"Then what is it, baby?" she questioned.

"I'm just so tired of dealing with no-good men, Mama. Why can't I find a good man to save my life?" As I cried out to my mom, thoughts of Rodney flashed in my mind of him working my body so sexually. He had that loving that kept me so unbalanced.

"Who done hurt you now?" She asked as if I had a hit list full of men.

I was silent as I shook my head, trying to erase him from my mind.

"Well, it really don't matter who it was. All that matters is that you hurt. Melody, you really need to just take some time out for yourself."

"Mom, I was celibate for two years. Don't you think that's enough time to be spending alone?" I was furious.

"Now, look here, don't you get snappy with me. I ain't the one who hurt you," she hissed.

"I'm sorry, Mama."

"Apparently two years wasn't enough 'cause you still running into the same problems."

"Mama, I'm thirty-five years old. I only have one child, and I want to get married before I die. I want to know what happiness feels like. I want someone to love me unconditionally. I want to go on romantic trips and long vacations with my man." I let out a deep sigh.

"I know you do, but you got to wait on the Lord to send you that right mate. It seems like the devil keeps blocking your blessings. You need to stop meeting these guys at the club. You need to let him court you before you give up the goods. Get to know him before you let him all the way in. Mel, I really think the problem is within. You need to stop looking and spend time with yourself. You so worried about getting married before a certain age. You have a lot of responsibilities when you become someone's wife. You need to make sure that you are ready to be married," she preached.

"I am," I said piping in. I knew once my mom started talking, it would be hard for me to get a word in.

"How you know you ready to be married, and you haven't even been in a long lasting relationship? What's the longest relationship you been in with a man?"

I acted like it was taking me a minute to think, but I already knew the answer. "Umm . . . six months."

"See there? You couldn't of known much about a person in six months. You might know how he like his eggs cooked and his favorite position during sex."

"Mom," I shrieked.

"Girl, I wasn't born yesterday. But seriously, you need to learn to love yourself before you start to even want to love a man. They know your weakness, and they know when you are vulnerable. Men know how to get what they want. And once they get it, they go on to the next one and stop treating you with respect. But if they see that you are not going to put up with their mess, then that's when they start acting right. I know you, Mel. You're my daughter. You can be very soft spoken at times, and you can also be a little naive. You need to work on yourself before you can find happiness in a man. Now, I'm not telling you this to hurt your feelings. I'm telling you this because I love you, and you deserve the best. You need to stop settling for less. You hear me?"

"Yes, Mama," I said softy, trying not to let her hear the tears in my voice. I was so sick of crying. I knew she was right. But only if it was that easy. I tried to get over Rodney, but he knew how to pull me back in. Mama was right when she said they know our weakness. I was definitely weak for him. I heard my phone beep, notifying me that I had a text. I pulled the phone from my ear and read the message. It was from Rodney.

Hey, babe, I wanted to call to let you know I'm all right, and I deserved what you did to me. I ain't mad at you. I love you. Please let me make it up to you. I wanna see you tonight.

I shook my head and put the phone back up to my ear.

"Mel, are you still there?"

"Yes, Mom, I'm listening. Why is God punishing me like this?" Warm tears fell from my eyes as I thought about how Rodney's words make me want to block everything out that my mom was saying to me.

"Child, hush, God's not punishing you. He don't work like that. Dry those tears, girl. I know you might get lonely sometimes, but when that time comes, read the Bible. God will never leave nor forsake you. Pamper yourself. You don't need a man to do nice things for you; you can do nice things for yourself. You need to just stop looking because you are using all of your energy trying to snag a man. For what? So he can leave you brokenhearted and miserable? You need to get back in church, but don't look there, because the men in the church are as bad as the men in the streets." She let out a giggle, and I followed right behind her.

It was good to talk to my mother. She was always there when I needed her, and I knew she would never tell me anything wrong. She always looked out for my best interest. I was going to stop being so soft spoken, and I was going to speak my mind and demand from Rodney what I wanted from him. Yes, I know my mom said not to look for a man. I'm not looking because I got Rodney. All I have to do is put my foot down and let him know that he better get his act together, because I deserve the best. I was sure that he would change after I tell him my good news. I have heard him talk about his kids, and even though they were grown, he still provided for them and is there when they need him. That's why I know that after I tell him that I'm carrying his seed, he will want to be there for me and our baby. I just had to get Kim out of the way. He needed to hurry up and get a blood test 'cause that baby didn't look like him at all. Rodney and I had put a lot of years into what we had, and I would do anything to make our relationship work. I'd be damned if I was about to be a single parent to another child. I was going to *make* Rodney love me.

24

Sasha

Melody had been pretty distant lately, so I decided to plan a lunch date for the two of us. I wanted find out what's been up with her. But I figure she was not talking to me as much because I visited Asia at the hospital only once. She needed to get over it. I didn't want to be all in Asia's face acting fake, because that ain't me. She was not dying, and the doctors said she would make a full recovery. We still didn't know what caused the accident. She ain't telling nobody. She didn't fall asleep at the wheel, so she knows how her SUV flipped over in the middle of the road.

As I walked in to Red Lobster, I saw Melody at a table that was alongside the wall. I bypassed the greeter with a smile and walked over to where Melody was sitting. The girl looked stressed out. Her eyes were puffy, like she'd been crying for days. Her hair was matted to her head like she had her curls out for a few days. "Hey, girl, I'm glad you were able to make it."

"Hey," she said as if she had no energy left in her body.

"Did you order yet?" I asked as I scanned the menu.

"Nope, I was waiting on you, but I know what I want." She took a sip from her ice-cold glass of water.

We ordered our food after the waiter came to the table, then waited for it to arrive. I couldn't stop looking at how pitiful Melody's face looked. I ended up telling her about how my mom treated me as a child, and I also told her that I told Jonathan that I was taking birth control without him knowing because I didn't want any children because I was afraid of being a bad mother. She was shocked, and she wondered why I had not told anyone sooner. And just like Jonathan, she said that my mom must have some type of disorder.

"Sasha, I really think you should have a talk with your mom. Because what she had done in the past is affecting your future. I think you would be a great mother." Melody always thought she could help everyone with her words. But I had not planned on speaking to my mom any time soon.

"I can't even fathom Aunt Arlene ever fracturing your arm and allowing you to suffer like you did." She showed sympathy on her face.

"Well, she did, because she's a nutcase," I huffed.

"But look at me trying to give you advice, and I can't even help myself." She swallowed hard and continued. "I have been in and out of bad relationships ever since I was old enough to date. I was just talking to my mom, and she asked me what the longest relationship I had been in was. It hurt me to tell her the longest one was six months. That's pitiful." Her eyes became glossy. "I didn't have a father role model when I was growing up, and that really affected how I dealt with the men in my life. I never knew how a man was supposed to treat a woman. I have been settling for lame, no-good suckers all my life. I blamed my father all these years, and I was feeling sorry for myself, but I also hated him for not being there to talk to me when I need a man's perspective. I always wanted to be a daddy's girl, but he was never there. Instead, he was in the streets either smoking dope or selling it. It depended on what type of week he was having."

Melody stared at her plate as if she was in a daze, but she wouldn't stop talking. She just wanted to get it all out, so I sat there and listened to her. "If his clientele wasn't contacting him for the work, he would get depressed and smoke up his supplies, then blame it on the devil. But when he was making money, he would come around dressed all fly, while I walked around looking like Raggedy Ann. Don't get me wrong, my mother keep me dressed nice, but it didn't compare to my dad's luxurious name-brand outfits, expensive shoe game, and his collection of fine leather and fur coats. And when he did come around, he had nothing for me, not even a decent conversation. And I hated him for that. I didn't ask for much. All I wanted was for him to love me. I'm his only daughter, his firstborn." Melody shifted in her chair; her face was filled with agony. While she spoke, I noticed that she barely touched the food on her plate.

It looked as if she wanted to cry. She was such a crybaby; she always cried at the drop of a dime. She reminded me of Kandi on *The Real Housewives of Atlanta*. When you looked at Melody the wrong way, she would cry. I felt bad for her because I knew how she wanted her dad to be around when we were younger. "I didn't have a mother or a father to give me love. I thought I was the only one that had it bad." I let out a deep sigh. I felt her pain.

"But the reason why I said that was because the way my father treated me in the past has affected how I am in my relationships with men, and what your mom has done to you in your past has affected your marriage. It's going to be tough, but we both need to forgive our parents and move on so that we can have a better life for ourselves." She cracked open the shell to her lobster tail, put the meat in her mouth, and looked at me for a response.

I just stared at her. I didn't think I would ever forgive my mother, but I was tired of talking about it, so I said, "Yeah, I'll work on forgiveness."

The table was silent until Melody asked, "How does your shrimp taste?"

"They're pretty good. You know, this is my favorite restaurant," I said as I put more shrimp in my mouth.

"Sasha, while you are working on forgiving your mom, you and Asia need to really make up. I mean, we are cousins for goodness' sake."

"We are not blood," I said calmly.

"Are you serious?" Melody spat.

"I don't have time for her fake behind. She was being slick when she hooked me up with David. She knew she had sex with him. She talking about she tried to stop me from leaving with him. She's a damn lie." I was angry, and I really didn't know why Mel had to bring her name up.

"Sasha, calm down. Asia didn't know you were going to sleep with him." She was nonchalant. That was like a slap to my face.

"Look, Mel, when I feel like talking to Asia, I will. I would rather talk about something else. I did not come here for this." I was straightforward with my words.

"Okay."

The table was silent once again.

"So what have you been doing lately besides working?" she asked with glee in her voice.

"Um . . . My life is boring. I've just been writing."

"For real! You still writing those freaky tales?" she smiled.

"Yup. And I love it."

"What do you get out of it? Don't you get . . . you know . . . horny writing about sex?" Melody giggled like a shy kid.

"I just have a wild imagination. I wish I could live out my characters in my books. Maybe that's the reason why I enjoy it. It's fantasy, but I love making it up 'cause I doubt if it will happen in my life. I wish I could find a young stud that would blow my back out every night." I smiled, but when I looked at Melody, her face was blank.

"What's the matter?" I asked.

"Oh, nothing," she stuttered. Then she cleared her throat. "Do you read a lot of erotic books?"

"Yes, I love Zane. Jonathan and I went to go see her new movie, and when they acted out the sex scenes, I was on the edge of my seat. I wish I could have been the main female actor. When I looked over at Jonathan, he had his eyes closed, like he was scared to watch." Melody laughed, but I was serious.

"She was bold. She stepped out of her natural comfort zone, and she was spontaneous and experimental. She was free. I just don't want to be too free and get AIDS like she did," I said.

"Do you miss Jonathan?" she asked unexpectedly.

"I miss him a little bit, but I don't want to be back with him. He wasn't giving me everything I needed. I know I cheated on him, but he didn't even comfort me when I told him why I didn't want kids. He wasn't even sympathetic toward my feelings when I told him I didn't think I would be a good mother because of how my mom did me. He is so insensitive, and I'm his wife. He doesn't really love me. All he wanted was a baby. And on top of that, I yearn for more than he was willing to offer. One day, I'll find a man that will give me what I need. He may have to be a young thang. He just better know how to handle these curves." I grinded in my chair to show her that I meant.

"Sex ain't all that if you not having it with someone that loves you. Jonathan loved you. You just better be careful for what you ask for," Melody said as a tear fell from her eye.

25

Melody

My mom really surprised me when she showed up to my door.

"Mom, what are you doing here?" I was in shock. I opened up the door and gave her a hug. "I'm so happy to see you." I couldn't stop smiling.

"Hey, baby. I wanted to come and get you out of this house. I know you have been going through some things, so I reserved us a room, just for you, Rayn, and me. We are going to have a little fun at a hotel and water resort."

"Are you serious? A water resort?" I smiled. I didn't think my mom would like something like that. Don't get me wrong. My mother was a very down-to-earth and pleasant person to be around. She was only hitting age fifty-one. With her toffee-colored wrinkle-free skin and her beautiful jet-black, naturally wavy hair, and with hips to die for, my mom had it going on. She, her sister, and brother lived only an hour away. They had all moved to take care of my grandmother when she became ill. She passed away a few years ago, and they all just stayed out there.

"Yes, a water park. I thought that would be fun for Rayn. And you and I can stay in the sauna," she smiled.

"Well, you know that Rayn will love that. Let me tell her you're here. Do you want something to drink while we pack?"

"No, I'm fine," Mom said. I rushed out of the room to get Rayn.

"Child, no need to rush. I ain't going nowhere. Just take your time." She took a seat on the sofa.

My mom and dad met in high school. They were in love, and my mom had me when she was seventeen years old. My grandmother was livid because my mom had a child out of wedlock and at a very young age. But she helped her out a lot. I was born around the time when the crack epidemic was tearing people's lives apart. My mother had a good job at the Jeep plant, and my dad was a mechanic. They were doing well for themselves . . . until they both got hooked on that mean drug, crack cocaine. If it wasn't for my grandparents, I don't know where I would be. My mother would leave me for days with my grandmother and aunts so she could go and get high. She went from working a good-paying job to losing it and working from job to job, barely paying the rent because she had to get her fix. We sometimes went without food in the house, but that's when my grandparents stepped in. They would buy food for me to eat. My dad's mother was also there for me, even when he wasn't.

My dad and mom broke up when I was three years old. That's when they both got addicted to crack cocaine. My father stayed in the same town, but I would never see him. I would stay over at my grandmother's house every weekend, and she would take me to family reunions with her. My dad wouldn't even come by to say hello. I always wanted to see him, and I always wondered why he didn't love me. My grandmother would just act like everything was normal and that her son wasn't in the wrong. But she would talk about how my mom was not a good mother because she couldn't keep food in the house. She had always been the one to show favoritism toward her own grown kids.

My mom struggled with trying to get herself clean for years. After going to recovery meetings, church, and staying in a recovery house, she kicked her habit when I was a sophomore in high school, and she never went back. That drug had control over my mom, but she was not a bad mom. She tried her best to get her life back on track. She had a disease that was ruining her life. She never abused me, and I had never seen her do drugs. She would smoke the pipe in the house, but she would be closed up in her bedroom. When I smelled the aroma from her room whenever she opened the door, I just thought she was smoking a funny-smelling cigarette.

I was a good kid. I had always done well in school, and I stayed out of trouble. But when I started junior high, that's when I started getting in to boys. I didn't have a father figure to tell me that he loved me, so when the boys gave me a little attention, I started falling in love and giving it up. Well, back then, I thought it was love. I would tell my mother I was going to track practice and tournaments, but I was really going over to some boy's house. I had never run track a day in my life. But she was so busy getting high that she didn't check to see what I was doing. When I was in high school, I had my first abortion, and that wasn't the last one. I had two after that. My mother never knew because I would get the money from my boyfriend at the time. Yes, I was a wild child, and I had lacked love from both of my parents.

After I had Rayn, my mom would help me with her a lot. She loved being a grandmother. Every summer, Rayn spent a month with her, and they have a ball. My mom always apologized to me. She would tell me that she wished that she hadn't put me through the things I had to go through in life. But I wasn't mad at her. I had seen worse things going on in my friends' households.

I couldn't even compare my life to theirs. Some of my friends were being abused or even raped by their own family members or their mothers' boyfriends. Their parents would smoke crack right in their face. I even had a friend tell me that she watched her mother give oral sex to a man for drugs. I was blessed because my life could have been worse. I had told myself a long time ago that I would never try any type of drugs, not even marijuana.

My mom met Rodney, and she thought he was a sweet guy, but she warned me that he was a little manipulative. I couldn't tell her that I was pregnant again without being married. But soon I would be married to Rodney, so I decided that I wouldn't tell her about the new baby coming until then.

"Nana, I'm all packed and ready to go," Rayn said, running down the stairs with glee. She had her duffle bag in her hand.

When we got to the resort we checked in to our room, and Rayn couldn't wait to go where the action was, so she put on her swimsuit, and Mom and I did the same.

"Now, Melody, we came here so you could relieve some stress. So we will not be bringing any negative thoughts or people into our conversations while were here, are we clear?" My mom gave me a reassuring smile.

"Yes, we are clear." I smiled back. I definitely didn't want to ruin my getaway thinking about the stuff I had been through.

Rayn was having a ball. She even met a few girls here, and they set it off. There were a few big waterslides and wave pools, and regular pools. I was glad that Rayn knew how to swim because some of the slides looked scary. I couldn't swim, so I knew I wasn't getting on them. After staying in the water for about three hours, we went to our room and ordered room service. It was really nice to lounge around with my mom and daughter for the weekend. I was enjoying myself.

"I'm so glad you two accepted my invitation to join me at this lovely resort," my mom said while lying in the bed resting.

"Nana, I wouldn't have missed it for anything in the world," Rayn said, and we all laughed.

"Mom, this was a great idea. Look at you . . . You still got it!" We all laughed again. I loved my family, and this is what we do. We pull each other out when they are going through something. We take care of each other. I just wished that Sasha and Melody would get their selves together. We had been tight all our lives; we are family, and they needed to forgive each other and move on. Life is too short to be acting the way they were acting.

Let me stop thinking about them. I don't want to mess up my vibe.

26

Sasha

I really didn't want to be here. But I was sitting in Amazing Grace Baptist Church, in a small room that was connected to the women's restroom with Asia's wedding party. We were all getting our makeup done by an independent consultant from Mary Kay Cosmetics. The chick knew what she was doing. Our finishing touches were flawless. She matched all the ladies up with the foundation that complemented our complexion perfectly, and she also added a light shade of fuchsia eye shadow on our brows. It went perfect with the fuchsia that was in our dresses that we wore for Asia's special day.

I had to give it to her. Asia did pick out some gorgeous dresses. They were tight fitted, long fuchsia halter dresses, with a thin black piece of fabric that draped in the front of the dress and was tied in the back in a bow. We all wore the same type of silver open toe stilettos. Asia was in another room getting ready. I hadn't seen her dress, but Melody was quick to tell me that she was going to look like a princess and that her dress was to die for. Melody had helped her pick out the dress. Asia knew she had better not ask me to meet up and help her with any of her plans. She should just be happy that I actually made it to join her wedding party. I so wanted to call Melody and tell her I was abducted by aliens, and I was on another planet, and I wouldn't be able to make it for the festivities.

Asia and I were still not on speaking terms. The last time I saw her was a few months back when I got fitted for my dress. She looked like a totally different person. That girl had always been overweight, and her body had always been disproportionate. But when I saw her, it looked like she had lost a good thirty pounds, and her face was filled with bags and stress lines. Maybe it was her kids giving her problems, or maybe she was jittery from all that she had to do with the wedding, but there was something going on with her. I wanted to give Asia a piece of my mind then, but she already looked busted and disgusted, so I didn't say anything to her, but best believe, there would be a time and place where I would confront her and tell her what a triflin' skank she really was.

Nevertheless, if I was not a part of this event, I would've never heard the end of it from my family. I was just trying to keep the peace, so I slowed up, and I'm staying out of the way. She'll be lucky if I get the urge to smile on her wedding picture. But since Melody is the photographer, she will probably not snap the photo if I don't smile. I wasn't looking forward to it. Speaking of Melody, that girl had been thorough hell and back over the past year. But I ain't gonna talk about her, because that will take up too much of my time. But let me tell you that shit hit the fan, babyyyy. Just wait until she speaks her truth.

Well, enough about Melody and Asia. I had finally met me a man that can take care of my sexual needs, and it's not Asia's leftover, David. Lamel and I have been dating for eight months, and he has really proved to me that a young man knows how to put in work. He is eight years younger than me. But age ain't nothing but a number. We have an open relationship, something like what Rodney and Melody had, but she just could never come to grips with it. I was cool with how our relationship was. We had an arrangement. I just made sure I used protection every time. I didn't want another marriage, baby, or any STDs.

I was living out my fantasy with Lamel. My erotica novel would be released in a matter of time. So look out, *Fifty Shades of Grey!* No, I had never read that book, nor had I watched the movie. But I had watched a few interviews that the author had done on YouTube. The author talked about how she needed to do research for the book. E. L. James, let me show ya how a sista gets down. I don't *need* to do research, because Lamel gets my creative juices flowing on paper *and* in the bedroom. What am I thinking about! We never "did it" in the bedroom. Yes, we were some freaks. We did not have "routine sex," like I had with Jonathan. We were spontaneous, and there was never a dull moment with us.

Lamel was sitting in the sanctuary. He told me when the wedding was over we were going to take a trip to the islands like *we* were the married couple going on their honeymoon. We were going to get our freak on in every room in the hotel and every beach on the island. Did I forget to mention that the brotha was paid? His family owns the highest-paid law firm in the area. Melody kept telling me that I should have tried harder to work on Jonathan and my marriage. She told me all I was thinking about was myself, and I should have respected him more. He kept telling me the same thing, but I didn't care what they thought, 'cause it was all about me.

After I saw my ex-husband (yes, I signed those papers) with another chick, I was done. She wasn't even cute, and she had a really bad shape. What was he going to do with that? Not a darn thang. I would have thought he would have got him a fly chick on his arm to make me jealous. But the Pop-Tart he was flaunting around like his trophy, his dime piece, looked like Halle Berry. Naw, fool, not the Halle Berry you see in magazine. I'm talking about when she played in the movie *B.A.P.S., that* Halle Berry. She was tore up from the floor up.

My mother had come in from out of town to be at the wedding. She kept calling me, but I kept dodging her calls. I wasn't ready to talk to her. I had to make sure I had a couple of shots of some very strong liquor before I could even think about giving her a minute of my time.

"Asia, come on, let me get a picture of you before you get in line to go out to the sanctuary," Melody said, pulling me from my thoughts. She was holding her camera, ready to shoot.

"Dang, hold up. I forgot my shoes in the car," I huffed. How could I forget my darn shoes?

"Girl, you better hurry up and get them before they start the music," she snapped.

I walked slowly out of the room on purpose. She knew I didn't care about being a part of this disarray. As I walked to my car, I saw Asia's soon-to-be husband arguing with some guy. He was fine. I couldn't hear what they were saying, but they were mad. I watched as they went back and forth with each other. It would be crazy if they would have got into a scuffle and the groom walked in the church with a black eye. I laughed to myself from that thought.

Then just like a feuding married couple, they stopped arguing and started chatting like the of best friends. I got my shoes out of my car and was about to go back in the church before Melody came looking for me. I gave the two guys one last gaze, and my shoes slipped from my grip because my whole body had gone limp. I couldn't believe my eyes. I had to blink twice and shake my head, hoping that would fix my impaired vision. But that didn't work because what I saw was really happening. Asia's soon-to-be husband, Steve, the man that she would be marrying within the hour, was tonguing down a man right in the church parking lot—in broad daylight.

"Wow, Karma is a bi—" I stopped myself because of where I was. Would I go in the church and tell my cousin, the one that I was mad at for introducing me to a man that she screwed, that her husband-to-be is on the down low, and that he is outside *locking lips with a man? "Nah, now* I think we're even. She had the nerve to try to drop the bomb on me. She just don't know that I *am* the bomb. I'm going to watch as her mess explodes in her face," I said out loud to myself. I then let out a devious laugh, picked up my shoes, and went into the church and took my spot in the line where the wedding party stood behind the closed doors of the sanctuary. The doors opened, the music started on time, and I smiled like a Cheshire cat as I strode down the aisle to the front of the church, where the pastor would soon wed the dysfunctional couple.

Part 2

27

Asia

It was an hour before my wedding. As I sat in the church's powder room getting my makeup done, I could feel the butterflies in my stomach. I was trying hard not to move while my beauty consultant finished the job. I was finally happy with the relationship I was in; I loved Steve and knew he loved me too. I would no longer be on the market, and I would no longer have to go around saying that I was single, because I was getting married.

"Asia, you can get up and see if you like it," Monica said after she applied lipstick to my thin lips.

I got up from the metal folding chair and walked over to check out my makeup. That particular mirror hung on a wall in the small powder room that was adjacent to the room where I would soon be changing into my gorgeous wedding dress. My makeup was flawless; my friend Monica had volunteered to give me and the bridal party a makeover.

I stared in the mirror in shock. I was speechless.

"Asia, do you like it?" she squeaked.

"Monica, I love it. I look so . . . beautiful," I cried out.

I was in awe. She had done a really good job. My eye shadow was a soft fuchsia pigment, the same color as my bridesmaids' dresses, and it covered the lids of my almond-shaped eyes. The blush on my cheeks really accentuated my cheekbones, and the plum color on my lips was gorgeous. In the past, the only makeup I wore was lip gloss, so this was a big change for me, and I loved it.

"I'm glad you like it. You're gonna be a beautiful bride." Monica's eyes sparkled as she looked at the work she'd done to my face.

I turned away from the mirror, let out a joyful smile, and gave her a warm hug. "I appreciate you."

"Yeah yeah yeah. I know you do. Now, let's get you into that beautiful dress." She grabbed my arm gently.

"Okay, let's go," I said as joy washed over me.

I couldn't stop smiling. This was my day, and I was going to marry the man I loved very much. He was my daughter's father. I was proud that I would finally be tying the knot and with a great, positive role model that all my kids could look up to.

Steve had been doing really well with the kids, considering the fact that we only conceived one of my three children together. My baby girl, Alexa, was conceived while he'd been locked up in jail. Even though he'd been upset when he got out, he understood that I didn't have to wait on him while he did time for his wrongdoing.

"Asia, your makeup is stunning," my mom said when I walked into the room where I would get dressed.

"Thanks, Mom," I smiled broadly.

"We only have thirty minutes, so let's get you in this dress," Mom said as she lifted the plastic from the gown.

Mom and Melody had been by my side, helping me to pick out the white chiffon, tight-fitted dress. The gown flared out at the bottom and had a jeweled collar that wrapped around my neck. It was also adorned with elegant jewels that wrapped around my waistline like a belt.

"Baby, that dress looks even more beautiful today than it did the day you tried it on." My mom's eyes glistened as she spoke.

"Yes, it really does fit nicely," I said, trying to hold the tears back.

I'd lost a few pounds because I was stressed out, hoping that the affair I'd been having with Lance didn't backfire during the time I was planning my wedding with Steve. Besides the car accident where Lance drove me off the road and the few unexpected phone threats he'd made about blowing up my house with me and my kids in it, I hadn't heard from him in a few months. I hoped it stayed that way. Even though shedding the extra pounds was very necessary, I didn't want to lose it *that* way.

"You are beautiful, but you better not cry and mess up the face I just took time to perfect," Monica snapped playfully, but I knew she was serious.

"I'm not going to cry," I smiled and dabbed the tears away. My hands shook, and my throat became dry. "I need some water." After a few sips, Monica retouched my lips and made sure that my tight Shirley Temple curls were placed just right.

"Are you ready to say your 'I dos' to the man you will promise to spend the rest of your life with?" Monica said as she lifted the tail of my dress so I could walk.

"Yes, I am." I exhaled, and then let out a slow breath. "I'm as ready as I'll ever be."

When I stepped out of my dressing room, my stepfather walked up to me, smiled, and said, "You are so beautiful."

"Thanks, Dad." My face beamed as we connected at the arms.

Dad wore a white tuxedo with a fuchsia vest and tie like the groomsmen. He was the only dad I knew. My mom told me that my biological father had died from a drug overdose when I was a young child. My stepfather had been very strict at times, but I knew he loved me.

As the doors of the church opened, I stood there for a minute to take it all in. The pews were packed with both

Steve's and my family and friends. My heart smiled from all the support we had on our big day. All the bridesmaids and groomsmen were looking spectacular as they stood in the front of the church.

The organist started to play, and at that very moment, my stomach contracted into a tight ball. Sweat trickled down from my armpit. I needed to get my nerves together.

"Asia, that's your cue to go," Monica said, breaking me out of my trance as she tried to hide so that no one in the sanctuary could see her. I knew that was my cue. Even though we had practiced this a million times at rehearsal, my feet were suddenly stuck like they were in quicksand. I knew it was just last-minute jitters, but when everyone stood up, and all eyes were on me, I shook the nerves off. That was when I started to take quick steps toward Steve as his cousin Paul belted out the words to Brian McKnight's song, "The Only One For Me."

"Slow down, baby, you're walking too fast," Dad said in my ear.

I slowed my pace, smiled, and knocked the anxiety from my mind as I tried to concentrate on the lyrics of the song Steve had chosen, a song Paul sang beautifully. After walking past the gorgeous fuchsia and white flowers that were attached to the end of each pew, the smiles that were plastered on the people's faces, and the lights that flickered from the cameras and cell phones as they captured images of me, I had finally made it to the altar. Standing next to Steve, I could tell he was as nervous as I was, but in his eyes, I could also see his love for me.

After we looked into each other's eyes and spoke our vows, we finally said I do. Then, we shared our first kiss as Mr. and Ms. Steve Goodwin. Unlocking lips, we turned toward the crowded sanctuary to walk out of the church—and that was when my heart fell from my chest to the floor, along with the bouquet of flowers that I'd been holding. I almost stopped breathing. From the way my husband looked at me, he must have thought I was stunned out of my mind. And he was right . . . because I was.

"Baby, what's the matter?" Steve asked with much concern.

Sweat dotted my temple. I swallowed deeply. I couldn't talk. My words were stuck in the back of my throat. My heart thumped hard in my chest as if it was about to burst. I blinked my eyes, hoping to clear my vision, praying that I wouldn't still see Lance sitting in the back of the church, eyeballing me with an evil glare.

28

Sasha

The deejay was playing "Let's Get Married" by Jagged Edge as the wedding party strutted into the elegant hall where the reception was being held. Asia's wedding had been really nice, but I was hoping some drama popped off. Especially after I'd seen her husband locking lips with a man in the parking lot right before they exchanged vows.

I thought Steve's lover boy would definitely be the one to stand up and object to the marriage, but unfortunately, everything went well. At least, until Asia looked as if she was having an asthma attack right before they exited the sanctuary—and the girl didn't even have asthma. I didn't know what was going on with her. All I knew was that she was bent over and having trouble breathing. I didn't know what Steve said to get her to straighten up, but I knew I would find out the four-one-one after she told Melody, because Melody would tell me. Asia and I still weren't on speaking terms, and I didn't care. I wasn't going to be fake and all up in her face.

I couldn't believe how her husband had said his vows to her so sincerely and innocently, like he hadn't just been slobbing down the throat of a man a few minutes earlier. I definitely had no plans on telling her that her husband was on the down low since she had no problem with hooking me up with a man that she had relations with. So, if she wanted to start, I was going to be the one to finish. But for her children's sake, I just hoped that man didn't give her AIDS while he was messing with men. I shook my head at *that* disgusting thought.

My young caramel latte was eyeing me throughout the ceremony, and I was googly eyeing him back the whole time. Yes, I and my young thang got turned up every night. Lamel was eight years younger than me, and he drove me crazy under the sheets. He was the total package. He sexed me good, he had good money, and he was good on the eyes.

He resembled Trey Songz with a smile that would make you weak in the knees, a tapered fade, a clean face, and a tight, muscular body with grown-man swagger that was to die for. He didn't act like a little boy like most of the men that had tried to run game on an independent, grown-ass woman like myself. He was confident, smart, and a businessman, helping his parents run their law firm. And did I tell you he gave me good sex?

His young ass loved it when I called him Big Papa. I thought it was corny at first, but I went with the flow because it seemed like he got excited when I moaned it out while he was pounding my brains out. He called me Ma. At first, I wasn't cool with my boy toy calling me that, but I went with it. That man was carrying a beef stick as long and thick as my arm. I would have called him whatever he wanted me to just as long as I got a piece of him on a daily basis.

I had to upgrade after I let Jonathan's punk ass go. I'd finally signed the divorce papers that Jonathan hand delivered to my door. He thought I was going to cause a scene, so he brought his cock-eyed mammie with him, and she sat in the car while he handed me the papers. That woman couldn't stand me, and I didn't give a flying fuck. I knew that she was overjoyed that her son and I were getting a divorce, but I didn't care about that either. In fact, I didn't want him, so he could stop thinking that I was about to fight for him. He just didn't know that I had met a man almost half his age, and he satisfied me completely. All my needs were met, and I had no time to think about Jonathan and his shenanigans.

Jonathan had wanted a baby so bad that, whenever we made love, he prayed while he stroked my body. "Lord, I'm about to give my wife a beautiful baby," he would growl as he arched his back and thrust his johnson deep inside of me. "Lord, please let this be the one," he would moan right before he released.

Then, he would just lie on top of me with his limp penis inside of me as if that would help his sperm swim to my ovaries. I would be so irritated with him that I would tell him to get his heavy, sweaty ass off of me. What man thought it was sexy to pray during sex? I was so over him that I couldn't wait to sign the papers to get him out of my life.

"Baby, what are you doing? Daydreaming? Let's dance," Lamel said as he pulled me from my thoughts.

"Okay." I smiled and took his hand as he guided me to the dance floor where we danced like we were the only ones on the floor. After a few songs, Lamel stated that he was hungry, so I told him to go over and have a seat at our table. I would fix him a plate, but I wasn't ready to eat yet.

The hall was decorated beautifully with tables that were the same colors as the wedding party apparel. As I walked up to the buffet, I heard a voice from behind me.

"Hey, beautiful lady. You sho'nuff sexy in that dress you wearin'," the husky, slurry voice announced. I turned around to see who it was. It was my mother's stepbrother.

"Uncle Bobby." I rolled my eyes and shook my head at him.

He squinted his eyes as he tried to figure out who I was. It took him a minute, but then he said, "Oh, you Arlene's daughter?"

"Yup." I gave him a half smile, but in my head, I was thinking, *You sho' look and smell a mess.* From the way his speech slurred, it seemed as if he had just downed a whole bottle of gin.

"What's up, niecey?" He smiled and gave me a warm hung. He called all his nieces that. I bet he didn't even remember my name.

Uncle Bobby was a dedicated alcoholic and crackhead. The last time I'd seen him, he'd been begging for change outside of a fast-food restaurant. I was pulling through the drive-through, and he didn't recognize me until I told him who I was. But that had been a mistake because as soon as he remembered me, he asked me for some money for food. I wasn't going to give him none of my money to go and smoke up. But I did ask him what he wanted to eat, and I bought it for him. "How are you doing? You're looking good," I lied, looking him up and down.

He was wearing a cheap, cream-colored suit with some Buster Brown, thick-soled shoes that looked too wide for his feet. Uncle Bobby had been a nice-looking, chestnut-complexioned brotha before he let the drugs add like ten years of stress to his face and body.

He stood about six feet, and he was lanky and frail. His hair was in a nappy, unlined 'fro, his face was sunken in, and he would have had a perfect smile if it wasn't for the tartar buildup on his teeth. But his almond-shaped, ebony-colored eyes were to die for. As a result of his former looks, back in the day, he was a ladies' man.

That wasn't his first time trying to run game on me. The last time was a few years back when we bumped into each other at a cabaret, and he was with his wife.

"I'm doing okay," he said, and his smile turned into a frown.

His wife had recently passed away from a heart attack, and the family was saying that he took her death really hard. She'd been the only person he had that he connected with because most of the family had disowned him because he couldn't control his addictions.

"You're looking nice," I lied. I wanted to cheer him up. I didn't want him jumping off the MLK Bridge because I'd brought up old memories.

"I'm gon' always be fly. I'm not a pimp, I'm a simp," he said proudly.

I scrunched up my face at his response. I wasn't going to even ask him what that meant.

"Alrighty, then," I said as I turned and started to fix Lamel's plate. My mom told me that Uncle Bobby was a little messed up in the head and that he could also talk your ear off.

"Niecey!" he said as he tapped me on shoulder. I turned to face him again, and he asked, "What do you do if you find a man that is about to retire?"

"Um, I don't know, Uncle Bobby. What should I do?"

"You should marry that fool!" he replied with an attitude because I didn't know the answer.

"Uncle Bobby, you're silly," I chuckled.

"Girl, I ain't silly. My wife had a good job. God rest her soul. But I'm still getting paid. I'm sixty-three, but when I turn sixty-five, I will be getting five hundred more dollars coming in." He said it as if the wind he let out with his words made him lose his equilibrium.

"Well, I'm glad you're making ends meet," I said as I walked a little farther away from him. I needed to get back to my date.

"Hey, Niecey, it was good seeing you again. I'm about to go find me a pretty young thang to dance with. Stay sweet, ya heard me?" He walked away with a staggered limp, not saying another word.

"Damn, baby. What took you so long? I saw you over there hollering at that old pimp," Lamel said with a crooked smile.

"That was my uncle." I gave him his plate, and he dug in like he hadn't eaten anything all day.

"That food was on point, but now, I'm ready for dessert." He stared at me and licked his lips.

"What's on your mind for dessert?" I asked seductively, because I already knew what his answer would be.

"You're always on my mind. And don't play with me, ma, because I will bend you over right here in front of all of your family members and have my way with you." He discreetly caressed my inner left thigh.

"Oh, no, you won't." I softy kissed his lips.

"Let's get out of here. I want to taste your other lips," he whispered in my ear. I giggled and instantly became wet between my thighs.

He grabbed hold of my hand and started to pull me away from the table. When he wanted to have sex, there was no stopping him. I never knew when or where he would just snatch my clothes off and devour my body. As we walked to the car, he pushed the button to start it. "You get in the driver's seat. I want you to drive so I can take care of some business," Lamel said as he opened the car door for me.

After he got in the car, I pulled off, not knowing our destination. "Where are we going?"

"Just drive." He turned around to face me. "Lift yo' butt up," he said when I stopped at the stop sign. I gave him a dumbfounded look. Then, he started pulling my dress up from the hem. That's when I realized that he wanted me to lift my butt up so that my dress could go up to my waist. After it was up enough to satisfy his needs, he said, "Drive."

I put my foot to the gas pedal. He slid his hand into my black lace thong, and I immediately panted like a dog in heat. I kept my eyes on the road, but I started to swerve just a little.

"Take control of that wheel while I put in work on this wet thang right here." He plunged his thick finger in and out of me, and my inner muscle clenched as the warm fluid oozed out. I released a slow moan as I relished his touch. I knew he wasn't done with me, so I headed to my apartment so we could finish what we started. But as soon as he noticed the direction I was going in, he started giving me the directions that he wanted me to go in. We ended up at the Grand Plaza Hotel located in downtown Toledo. He got the honeymoon suite on the rooftop.

"I know we just left your cousin's wedding, but let's pretend this is *our* honeymoon, and you saved yourself for this day. Act like this is your first time. Let's start over there in that sauna, then we can make our way outside to the rooftop." Lamel placed soft butterfly kisses all over my face. My body shook uncontrollably. I was filled with burning lust, and I felt unbalanced just imagining what was about to go down.

29

Melody

I lay in my bed and thought about how I had been so out of character; I didn't know who I was. It all started about five months ago. Rodney and I were doing our thang, but when he wasn't around, I would crave for his touch. Since I couldn't get it from him, I started having late-night creeps with a few of my exes. I couldn't believe I was wild'n out like I was. I went from sleeping with one man to screwing three men in two weeks. I needed to stop that behavior, and so, I did. I shook my head with disgust at the person I had become. I felt like a nasty whore. I was raising a daughter. What if she had found out I was acting like that? My phone ringing brought me back to reality.

"What's up, babe?" Rodney said jauntily into the phone like we had spoken recently. Like he had no care in the world; like his life was just peaches and cream.

"What's up?" I said dryly, making sure he heard the irritation in my tone.

"What's wrong with you? I've been noticing lately that you ain't been wanting to see me. What, are you all up in your feelings again?" he asked, now sounding sincere. Rodney and I had not seen each other in about two months. I had been dodging him for two reasons. First of all, he still had not gotten the blood test back for the baby that was still living under his roof. And second, I was hiding because I was four months pregnant. Last time I saw him, I was not showing, but since I was craving everything under the moon, I was gaining weight. I wore baggy clothes because my daughter and my family didn't know that I was pregnant, and I wasn't ready for them to know yet.

"I'm just so over you. I'm so sick of your lies and the bullshit you be putting me through. I'm just sick of you!" I grunted. What I said was true. I wished I would've made the decision to stop dealing with his bull months ago. Then I wouldn't be in the predicament I was in.

"Babe, you know you miss me. Let me come over. I haven't got none of that good-good in a minute. You've got me over here going through withdrawals like a mutha," he said seductively. He was so conniving, but I fell for his ass every time. I blew out a deep sigh as I thought about the mess I was in. I had taken it upon myself not to purchase the morning-after pill that he'd given me the money for the morning after we had unprotected sex. My crazy in-love ass thought that it would be a good idea that I not terminate my pregnancy, hoping that the baby would help our relationship. Even though I had not told Rodney, I was beginning to realize that was the dumbest thing I could have ever done.

I wasn't no high school chick; I was a grown woman, and I knew that I shouldn't have become pregnant by a man that wasn't my man, a man that didn't even know I was carrying his baby. But it was too late. I didn't believe in abortions, and the baby was coming no matter how Rodney felt about it. I just hoped he would forgive me for holding the pregnancy from him. And I still hoped that the other alleged baby wasn't his.

"Mel, are you still there? I'm on my way, so we can talk," Rodney said.

"Whatever. I know what you want when you say you wanna talk," I spat.

He burst into laughter. "Don't act like you don't want it like I do."

Any other time when he said those words, I would jump up with joy because I knew he was about to come and give me the business. But after all the time we put into what I wanted to be a faithful relationship, something that was not what he wanted, I was tired and starting to get over him. I didn't want his sex.

"Whatever, Rodney," I moped. I knew he was going to come over, and it was time that I told him the truth. Well, hell, I didn't have to tell him a thing. All he had to do was look at me to see that I was with child.

"Okay, I'm on my way. Put on that sexy red thang that I like," he chuckled, and then hung up the phone.

I had gained about twenty pounds and was starting to show it in my face, belly, and thighs. The last time Rodney came over, he noticed I was getting thick, but he just thought it was from eating.

"Damn, baby, the last few times we went out to dinner, you've been smashing. But I ain't mad; you're looking good with that extra weight. Look at that ass. Let me get a hold of that," he said as he took both of his hands and squeezed my backside.

That night I was kinda scared that if he saw my stomach, he would know. I wasn't ready to tell him, so I turned the lights off and let him hit it from the back until we both reached our point of ecstasy. Then, he pulled out.

I wanted to tell him the damage was already done and that he had no reason to pull out now. Instead, I got up from the bed and took a long shower. When I got out, I was glad to see he was gone. In the past, he would never leave, but I took a long shower on purpose because I knew he was a very impatient person. I didn't want to get dressed in front him, so while I was in the shower, he told me that he was leaving, and I told him bye.

When he got to my house tonight, I wasn't gonna beat around the bush. I was going to tell him why I did what I did. And if he loved me like he said he did, then we would work through it together.

30

Asia

As my husband and I walked in the warm white sand at Orient Bay in St. Maarten, I was stunned at how beautiful the Caribbean island was. The enticing island was filled with flaming bright red, orange, and yellow flamboyant trees. I had never seen anything like it. Our days were filled with sunshine, velvet soft nights, and breathtaking scenery.

"Babe, are you ready for a swim?" I asked my husband as my feet enjoyed the heat of the powdery white sand with every step I took. It was so relaxing. But I wanted to get in the water again and feel the turquoise water massage my cares away. Early that day when we got in, I didn't want to get out. It felt like heaven.

"Yes, let's get back in," Steve said as he lifted me up and carried me in the water. I wrapped my arms around his neck, and once we got in the water, I kissed him passionately. I wanted to make love to him like we did the night before on the beach, but it was broad daylight now. Not having the kids around was great. I was able to be free and make love to my husband the way I wanted to with no interruptions. My thoughts went back to the night before.

***

"Babe, let's go on the beach and take this bottle of wine with us. There's no one out there, so we can let the alcohol take us wherever," Steve said as we stood on the balcony of our honeymoon apartment and looked out at the water.

We stayed at La Plenitude, which was located in the peaceful neighborhood of Friars Bay. La Plenitude was comprised of two buildings with six apartments in the middle of a big woodland park. The decor had been carefully chosen to immerse us in a peaceful and harmonious atmosphere.

Our apartment had a kitchen on the terrace that we never used because we always ate at whatever restaurants we passed by. We had a large bathroom, with a dressing room, and the bedroom was gorgeous, with bright beige walls, light-colored ceramic tile floors, and a huge bed that would fit an army. There was no TV or phone in the room on purpose so that we could enjoy the tranquility undisturbed.

I was excited to hear Steve say that he wanted to be naughty on the beach. I got the bottle of wine, and we walked through the quiet park to the beach. It was three in the morning, and there were no bystanders. After we talked and sipped on the wine on the blanket that Steve laid out for us, he whispered in my ear, "Do you want to make out right here, right now?" I could tell he was feeling himself.

I giggled at his playfulness. "What if someone sees us?" I asked nervously.

"We can make it quick. This sand, this beach just does something to me. I want to fuck the shit out of you right now and capture the moment on this beautiful island with my stunning wife," Steve said seductively as he cuffed my face in his hands, and then kissed me forcefully.

My body started to tingle in all the right places. He then took his tongue and licked my neck, down to my breasts; then he quickly pulled my sundress up. He took his moist tongue and maneuvered it down my stomach to my sweet spot. Then, he went to town eating me like he was eating the last meal of a dying man. I went crazy because it felt so good to be making love on the sand on the beach as I looked up at the stars that sparkled in the dark sky. I had never had anything this amazing happen to me, and I was on cloud nine. "Oh, baby, you're about to make me cum," I purred as I grabbed hold of his head tightly.

After I released my juices, I returned the favor to my husband until he burst out of pure ecstasy. Then, we finished what we started back in our room.

The next day, we were on the beach again and enjoying the sunset. I don't know what made me think about the crazy shit that went down at our wedding, but I couldn't block the fact that Lance was a crazy muthafucka from my mind. After I saw him chillin' in the sanctuary of the church, I couldn't leave the States quick enough. What the hell was wrong with him? He was psycho for real. What in the world had I gotten myself into?

After we'd connected at the eyes, it felt as if my heart stopped, and I thought I would pass out. But after Steve looked at me with panic in his eyes and asked me what was wrong, I had to straighten up. I didn't want to destroy what was supposed to be the happiest day of our lives. I inhaled deeply, and then lied and told Steve that I felt light-headed because I was too excited to eat anything. He kissed me on my cheek, picked me up, cradled me in his arms, and walked us out to the black Hummer limo. I didn't look back. Instead of everyone congratulating us outside of the church after the ceremony, Steve told the pastor to announce to our guests that we would greet everyone at the reception.

Steve told the driver to stop at the corner store. He wanted to run in and get me something to munch on so that I would have enough energy to make it to the reception after we took pictures outside of the Toledo Art Museum. Before we headed to the hall to eat some real food, half of the bridal party got out to purchase their own beverages, even though the limo came with three bottles of wine.

When Steve got out, I panicked as I looked out the window. I wanted to make sure that Lance wasn't following us. While everyone was dancing, laughing, and drinking as the limo drove around town, I tried to keep a smile on my face. My knees trembled under my dress as I prayed silently that Lance wouldn't show up at the art museum or reception. He didn't, and everything went well. My family show up and showed out. I had a ball, and everything was perfect . . . from the gorgeous photo shoot that Melody did, to the beautifully decorated hall where the reception was held. That was a day I would cherish forever.

"Honey, you really look nice in that swimsuit," Steve said, breaking me from my thoughts. After our swim, we ended up walking to a bar made of straw that was located on the beach. We were sitting at a small round table sipping on frozen daiquiris.

"Thank you," I blushed.

I had lost about thirty pounds. Steve thought that I lost it for the wedding, but the truth was that I was stressed out. Every day, I thought Lance would get in contact with my husband and fill his head with lies that would destroy what we had. Steve and I were happy, and the children enjoyed having a father at home. He took my oldest son to basketball practice, and we did things together as a family, something that my kids weren't used to.

I wished I could tell Steve about Lance, but I didn't know what Lance was capable of doing ever since he drove me off of the road. He could pop up anywhere and harm my family. I wished I could do something that would just get rid of him with the quickness. Every day, I feared for my life, and I didn't like living like that. I was living a nightmare, and all I wanted to do was wake up and my life would be back to normal—like it was before I bumped into Lance at the meat counter at the supermarket.

31

Sasha

After Lamel and I had crazy sex in the hotel, we slept like we had worked a twelve-hour shift. He was amazing, and he knew it. When I was with him, I felt younger. I was energized and spontaneous, and I loved it. There were no limits to what we did, and I never knew what to expect with him. He was my knight in shining armor, but we weren't attached at the hips, and that's the way I liked it. When I wanted to be alone, he wasn't clingy. He gave me my space.

Lamel had money. He worked at his parents' law firm, which was one of the best in the state. He was also one of the top lawyers in the company. We met when I was searching for a lawyer to handle my divorce. I was attracted to him because of his confidence, but he was also smart, successful, and handsome with swagger that was on point. Money was never an issue. If one day he wanted to fly me on a private jet or rent a luxury yacht, he would make it happen like it was nothing.

I checked my phone after Lamel dropped me off at home and saw that my mother had called me several times. She had tried to talk to me at the reception, but I acted as if I was too busy entertaining Lamel so she would leave me alone. She left me messages saying that she wanted to talk to me before she left to go back to Michigan.

We had not talked since I left home for college. I wanted to see what excuse she would give me for not wanting to be in my life. But deep down in my heart, I knew she didn't want me, because if she did, she would've never treated me the way that she did while I was growing up. However, it was time to stop running from my past and see what she had to say. I decided to call her back, and I told her that she could come by my apartment so we could talk.

I straightened up to make sure everything looked nice. This was my mom's first time visiting me after Jonathan and I divorced. As a matter of fact, she never visited the home that he and I shared. I knew the first thing she would want to talk about would be my failed marriage. I was going to tell her what she wanted to know, and I wasn't going to beat around the bush. After I wiped the glass table with Windex, I heard the doorbell ring. I placed the Windex back in the cabinet under the kitchen sink.

I looked in the large, rectangular mirror that hung over my leather sofa to make sure my hair was in place; then I smoothed out my collar. I don't know why I was nitpicking and taking my time to answer the door. That woman had not been in my life for years. Why was I worried about what she thought? She wasn't the least bit worried about me.

Before I walked toward the door to answer it, I looked over the apartment to make sure everything was presentable.

"Hey, Sasha," was what my mother said when I opened the door. She showed no expression, so I gave her none.

"Come in." I took two steps to the left so she could enter. After she made her way in, I closed the door and walked behind her as she looked around my small apartment.

She looked so different from the last time I saw her. Her skin tone was the color of sandpaper; it looked coarse and rough. She was slimmer than before, and the clothes she wore sagged.

When I was at the wedding, I was too busy trying to avoid her, so I really didn't get a good look at her. We hadn't seen each other in about fifteen years. That was a long time not to see the person that gave birth to you. But my mother was very cruel to me when I was younger, and I couldn't wait to get out of her house.

"This a small place you've got here." She flopped down on the red, leather sofa. Then she looked up at the skylight and the fireplace. "But it's nice though."

"Thanks. Do you want something to drink?" I huffed as I looked down at her as I stood over her.

"Yeah, what you got?" She pulled her purse strap from her shoulder and set it next to her. "Pepsi, bottled water, and um, Kool-Aid," I said, trying to think of what I had.

"Pepsi with ice would be good."

After I got her drink, I got myself a water and sat on the love seat across from her. She took a sip of her Pepsi and said, "So, Sasha, why are you living in this small apartment when I heard you were living large with that man you married?" She said it as if she was scolding me like I was a child.

Wow, is she really coming at me like that?

She had made me mad already, and she had been in my presence not even ten minutes.

"First of all, that man I married wanted to keep the large house that we had. I got this small apartment because it fits my needs. I don't need a large space; I'm single, and I'm loving it," I spat back at her. I knew she didn't think she was going to come to my home and stomp me down in my shit. She was starting already, and I was ready to kick her ass out. She had always been so judgmental and nerve-racking. She said she'd heard I was living in a large house because that woman never came to visit me. She didn't even come to my wedding, or for my baby girl's birth or home-going service. She was only in town because of Asia's wedding. I was grown now, and I wasn't going to bite my tongue. I had some stuff that I needed to get off my chest.

"You don't have to get sassy with me; I'm still yo' mother." She sat up as if she would charge at me if she had to. I didn't flinch a bit; I was ready for whatever. I had lost respect for her the day I left her house.

I rolled my eyes and said, "So, you decided to come by to talk to me now. Why?"

"What do you mean, why? You are my daughter, and I wanted to see you. I haven't seen you since you left for college and—"

"Yes, fifteen years ago. Now, you want to see me. Why?" I asked again, cutting her off.

"What happened to your marriage?" she asked as she took a sip of her drink like she was unfazed and couldn't be bothered enough to answer my question.

"You know what happened! I know you talked to Jonathan about what happened. You talked to my ex-husband over the phone more than you ever talked to me. And why does it matter anyway? It's over. So, it's really too late to be concerned now." I looked her dead in the eyes and waited for her to respond.

"Yeah, we talked a few times, but I want to hear from you. You know, it's always two sides to a story." She took another sip of her drink. She was talking to me like she was interviewing me, like I was on *Oprah* or something. Why was she acting like she cared so much?

"Since you ain't gonna drop it, we got a divorce because he wasn't satisfying me like I needed him to. He was selfish, and he wanted another baby, and I didn't," I said nonchalantly. Then I sat back and crossed my legs.

"Oh, is that what happened?" she asked in shock, as if she heard something different.

"Yup, that's what happened, and I'm not looking back. So, don't come up in here telling me that I need to try to work it out because I ain't," I barked. I was sick of Melody and everyone else saying that Jonathan was the best thing that ever happened to me, and I should have made it work between us.

"Gal, you sho' got a lot of anger in you. I just wanted to make sure I heard yo' side. Yo' ex called me on the phone and told me that you was the selfish one and that you didn't respect him as yo' husband or the man of the house. He also said that you kept a secret from him that you were on birth control when you knew he wanted a baby." She looked at me with raised eyebrows, waiting to hear what I had to say.

"Well, he's a liar. I told him that I didn't want any more babies, and he just didn't know how to respect my needs," I huffed. I took a sip from my water. I was getting heated and ready to end the conversation. Why in the hell were we talking about a man I was no longer involved with? Why in the hell was she coming at me, questioning me over some nonexistent shit?

"But why don't you want more children, Sasha?" she asked with a concerned expression on her face.

Is she serious? Is she really asking me that dumb-ass question?

"I didn't want to have kids because I didn't want to end up being a horrible mother like you." I shifted in my seat. Oh, I was pissed. I was also hurting inside, but I wasn't going to let her see my pain.

"What do you mean you didn't want to be a horrible mother like me?" Her face was filled with confusion at first, and then anger washed over her.

"What, now you've got amnesia? Don't sit here and act like you don't remember locking me in closets and keeping me there for hours."

Her mouth dropped open, and her eyes popped out of their sockets from shock. "Oh my God! Please say it ain't so."

She was dead serious; she didn't remember what she had done to me. "Mom, are you sitting here telling me that you don't remember locking me in the closet while you sat nearby on the sofa and watched TV? I could hear you laughing and talking to the TV. I would be in the closet for hours, and you told me that the reason why you did what you did was because you didn't want the 'bad people' to get me. I would scream and cry and beg you to let me out. But the more I beat on the door and called out for you, the more you ignored me."

I looked at my mother, and her face was drenched in tears. I was now the one confused. I got up and gave her a Kleenex that I got from my purse because there was snot running in her mouth. I had a weak stomach, and I didn't want to see that shit. Her hand shook as she grabbed the tissue.

"Baby, I'm so sorry. I had no clue why you carried so much anger toward me when you were young. All this time, I just figured you didn't want to be bothered with me because maybe you were going through a phase that teens went through. I would try to ask yo' aunties what I should do to bring you around. They told me that you never gave them any problems when you went to their homes to stay with Asia and Melody. You always seemed to want to get away from home and stay with them. Now I know why." She took the Kleenex and wiped her nose; then she continued. "Please, tell me you're not making this up. Please tell me that I didn't do those horrible things that you said I did," she pleaded.

I had begun to cry because she truly didn't remember. "Mom, are you telling me that you also don't remember telling me that the devil was in my soul? Then you tried to shake it out of me. You shook and yanked on me so hard that you fractured my arm. You made me sleep in agonizing pain because you didn't want to take me to the doctor. You thought that the bad people would take me from you." Tears continued to fall from my eyes, and I looked at her expression. She was shaking her head no as if she was having a seizure.

"No, no, no! I couldn't have done that to you!" she sobbed. Then she put her head down and said, "So, the doctor *was* right. I thought that doctor was making it up. I thought that doctor was using me as a guinea pig when he told me that he wanted to test me. No one had ever told me that I did strange things like what you are telling me, so I didn't believe him when he told me that I was diagnosed with schizophrenia."

I gaped in stunned silence as my jaw dropped. Jonathan and Melody were right. All this time I thought that my mother didn't want me, she was ill. She was schizophrenic.

32

Melody

Rodney didn't show up like he said he would last night. I was tempted to go over to his house, but I didn't. I got up out of the bed and saw Rayn off to school. Then I decided that I was going to have a worry-free day. I knew that all the stress I was going through was not good for the baby.

I had made an appointment to get my hair done. I needed some me time, and I was tired of walking around looking ugly. If my mom was here, she would've let me have it because I wasn't keeping myself up. She always told me I should look my best, even if I was only going to the corner store. If she would've seen me at that moment, she would've had a heart attack. My hair was dry, dirty, and I was way overdue for a steam treatment. The back of my head looked like a Brillo Pad. I was trying my best to keep my hair natural, but it was a lot of work to keep it up. I was two steps away from going back to getting a relaxer. We naturals called it the creamy crack for the hair.

I searched my walk-in closet for something comfortable to wear. My belly was poking out a little, and I needed to go shopping for bigger clothes. I found a pair of pink jogging pants that I got from Pink, and then found the shirt to match it. I walked out of the closet and stood in the mirror and lifted my shirt to see my belly bump. I shook my head at the fact that I had a baby growing inside of me and no one knew. They didn't know because I was too ashamed to tell them. I promised myself and my family that I wouldn't have another baby out of wedlock, and look at me—pregnant again. And my baby's daddy wasn't ready to be in a committed relationship. A single tear fell from my eyes because of the situation I was in.

I took a shower to relax my body. I let the pellets from the lukewarm water soothe my burning soul. After I got out of the shower, I put on my clothes and took another look in the mirror. When I had clothes on, you couldn't even tell I was pregnant, so I guessed that would give me more time to kill before I told my family. As soon as I saw Rodney, though, I was gonna let him know.

I walked into Genesis Hair Salon, and before I took a seat, I walked over to my hairstylist's booth and waved at her to let her know I had arrived.

"Hey, boo. I'll be right with you as soon as I wrap her and put her under the dryer," my beautician, Deedee, announced. I walked back over to the waiting area and sat down. The area was very small; it was located by the front entrance. The one thing I hated about sitting in the front was that the customers had to get buzzed in before they could enter. Every time I went to get my hair done, someone would ring the bell, and it would take forever for one of the beauticians to buzz them in. Then when they finally were able to enter, they glared at the people that were seated and gave us a look that read *you know you could have opened that damn door.*

I sat there patiently waiting for Deedee to call my name as I looked at this little girl. She had to be about six years old. I assumed she must have been waiting for her mother to finish getting her hair done. Her hair was freshly done with small French braids plaited into two ponytails. As I admired her hair, I thought about Rayn when she was that age. Boy, how time flies. My baby was turning thirteen. I was blessed to have such a smart, athletic, and respectful daughter. I just prayed that she didn't follow my path and end up dealing with good-for-nothing-not-knowing-what-they-wanted men. The doorbell ringing pulled me out of my thoughts. When they finally buzzed the person in after about three minutes and four rings, I was shocked to see the face that entered into the building.

"Hey, Tasha." I spoke in a cheerful manner as my heart beat to a fast pace. I didn't think I would run into her today.

"Hello." She looked at me as if she didn't remember where she knew me from.

"I'm Melody. Rodney introduced us at the club awhile back."

She smiled and said, "Oh, hey. I was trying to figure out where I knew you from. I haven't seen you in a while." Tasha was Rodney's sister.

That's because I've been busy stressing over your brother. "Yes, I've been busy with my business and with my daughter's sports and stuff." I kept a friendly smile pasted on my face.

"Oh, that's cool. Well, let me go and tell my beautician that I'm here, and I'll be right back," she said as she walked to the back. She was an attractive dark-skinned, plus-size chick. She had flawless skin, and she always dressed nice. She was older than me, but I didn't know her age. Rodney really didn't talk much about her. All I knew about her was that she had two young boys, and that she worked as an administrator at a daycare center.

When Tasha came back to the waiting area, she sat right next to me. "So, how have you been doing?" She crossed one leg over the other and sat up straight in her chair.

"I'm good. How about you?" I said with a forced smile. I kept it short because I wasn't going to tell her how I really felt.

"I'm good, life is good. When was the last time you saw my knucklehead brother?" she asked without taking a breath. I knew that was coming.

"Um, I talked to him yesterday." I was becoming uncomfortable. I wasn't used to talking to her, so I didn't want to get too personal, but I did want to pick her for information about my baby's father.

"Well, that's cool. I'm glad y'all are still cool. I know he's got some crazy shit going on in his life. But he talked about you in the past, and he really cares about you." She smiled jauntily at me.

He really cares about you. Those words made my heart smile. I knew Rodney cared about me; we'd been through a lot of stuff together. It was just good to hear someone else say it for a change.

Then I wondered what she was talking about. Rodney and I hadn't really discussed anything he was going through. He was kind of distant with me, and I didn't want to pry information from him. I just thought he would talk to me when he felt like it. I didn't want to run him away. He knew I was there for him when he needed me.

"Yeah, we've been talking, and he said he was becoming overwhelmed with the situation he was in," I lied, trying to push more information out of her.

"So, you know about ol' girl?" she asked me with questioning eyes.

Is she talking about the chick that's been living with him? "You're talking about the girl that's staying with him?" I asked, hoping she would tell more.

"Damn, y'all must be real tight for him to tell you about what's going on. So, he told you that the chick ain't trying to leave? My brother is crazy 'cause he just won't put her out. They got the blood test back, and the baby is not his, so I don't know why he just don't put her out. She's got some type of hold on him. He tells me that he cares for you. I always tell him that he needs to get his act together because he's too old to be—" She paused. Then she said, "He needs to just get his shit together." I knew she wanted to say that he was fuckin' around, but she stopped herself because that was her brother.

I was also glad to know that the blood test confirmed that the baby wasn't his. I wanted to jump for joy, but I didn't. I stayed calm and collected. So, Rodney was telling me the truth when he said he didn't want her there, but I already felt that in my heart because that whore wasn't even cute. He just felt sorry for her, and he's got a good heart, so he wasn't gonna put her and her baby out in the streets. But I was going to do something about that situation real quick.

I wanted to smile, but I didn't because I didn't want her to see my emotions. "He just doesn't want her to be on the streets," I confessed. That's what he told me. I looked at Tasha, and it looked as if she wanted to say more. I tried to give her time to say what was on her mind, but then Deedee called me to her chair. *Damn!* Tasha told me to give her my number so that we could do lunch some time or just kick it. She locked my number in her phone, and I went to get my hair done up.

33

Asia

Our honeymoon was over, and I had a great time on the island with my hubby. I never imaged it to be that beautiful. It was like paradise, and I didn't want to leave. If it weren't for the kids, Steve and I would've stayed a few more days. But they were blowing my phone up because they couldn't wait to hear how much fun we had, and they were excited to see what we brought back from the island for them. Steve and I had to purchase another suitcase to pack all the souvenirs we bought for the kids. I couldn't wait to see their faces when they got their gifts.

When we made it home, I decided to take the kids to their favorite spot, Chuck E. Cheese's. They hated that we were gone for a week, but they did enjoy spending time with my mother and stepdad. I hadn't talked to Melody and Sasha since I came back in town, so I told Melody that I wanted to hook up with them so I could tell them about my trip. Melody said that she would let Sasha know and that we could meet at San Marco's, a Mexican restaurant located on the south end of town. They had good food and the best margaritas in the city.

Sasha and I had been distant ever since I hooked her up with David. David and I had spent one night together in college, and we had just been cool after that. When I saw him in the club eyeballing Sasha, I told him who she was, and they ended up getting together. I didn't think that Sasha's married ass was going to go home with him, but she did, and I guess that's what caused her divorce. But I was going to be the grown up about the situation and apologize to her. Life was too short, and we needed to squash it. Besides, I heard she had a new guy in her life, and I was happy for her. Now that I had my husband, I wasn't mad at her anymore for marrying my high school crush. Everything was good; Sasha and I could get back to how things used to be between us.

I left the kids with Steve and jumped into my car to go meet Melody and Sasha. I decided to dress casual with a pair of stonewashed jeans and a black shirt that had FLAWLESS printed across the front. When I walked into the restaurant, I saw Sasha. She just gave me the stank face right before Melody got up to give me a hug.

"Hey, girl. You're lookin' cute," Melody said.

"Thanks, you do too," I said. I knew that Sasha wasn't feeling me, but I didn't give a damn. I went over to her and gave her a one-armed hug since she didn't get up from her seat. It was time to squash the beef, and it looked like I was gonna be the one to mend our relationship.

"Did y'all order y'all's food yet?" I asked.

"Nope, we were waiting on you," Melody answered as she took a sip from her drink.

"What you drinking?" I asked as I picked up the menu from the table.

"Girl, I don't know. I forgot what the waiter said this concoction was. I told her to give me the best cocktail drink, and she brought me out this. It's pretty good too." Melody smiled and took another sip. Sasha was looking at her phone as if we weren't even sitting at the table together. *So rude.*

After the waiter took our order, we chitchatted about the wedding.

"Yo' wedding was the shit. Everybody came out to support you. I was shocked to see Uncle Bobby's old-school ass up in the mix. He looked a hot mess," Melody laughed out loud.

"Leave that man alone. He just loss his wife; he's probably still mourning," I said.

"Girl, he probably is, but he knew he could have put together something else to wear. That suit was outdated when Ronald Reagan was president," Melody said, and we all burst out laughing.

"But on a serious note, I'm so happy that you and Steve finally tied the knot. It seems like he's a much better dude since he got out of prison," Melody said as she chewed her food.

"Yes, he is a good dude, and the kids love him. As long as my kids are happy, then I'm happy. But I do love him; he's getting his shit together. His business is booming, and he's such a caring and giving person. So, yes, he has changed a lot," I said.

"What's going on with your love life, Sasha?" Melody asked.

Sasha raised her eyes from her food and said, "Girl, I'm living my life like it's golden. As a matter of fact, Lamel and I are going to Jamaica in a week," she boasted.

"Are you serious? Damn, girl, he must have a lot of money for y'all to be goin' way out there," Melody spoke with excitement.

"Yeah, he's paid. I told you that his parents owned a law firm." She smirked with confidence.

"I know you're gonna have fun. I wish I had someone to take me somewhere out of Toledo. Shit, I would be satisfied with a trip to Chicago. Anywhere. I ain't hard to please," Melody moped.

Melody looked as if she was gaining weight. I noticed her face was a little fuller, and her hips were spreading. I hoped it was just food and not pregnancy. From the last I heard, she and Rodney were still not on the same page. Let my mama tell it, they weren't even in the same book. My mother and Aunt Darlene were always talking, and my mother knew how to get things out of people before they even knew that they had slipped and told her.

"Melody, you sure are looking good with that extra weight you put on." I smiled.

Melody's eyes widened, and she swallowed hard. In a nervous tone, she said, "Thanks."

That heffa *was* pregnant. I wanted to say something, but I didn't. When she was ready to tell us, she would. I hoped she wasn't hiding it because she was planning on having an abortion.

The table was quiet while we finished our food, and Sasha still hadn't said a single word to me. "Sasha, I want to apologize to you about the incident with David. We were cool in college, and what we had wasn't nothing. I just thought it would be cool to introduce y'all when he asked me who you were. I didn't have enough time to tell you that we had hooked up once back in the day." I spoke sincerely.

"Girl, please. Why are you bringing that up? That was so yesterday. I ain't thinking about that man and what y'all had. My life is good, and like I said, my man and I will be taking a private jet away from here. I can't be happier about the space I'm in now."

Sasha was definitely giving me attitude, but I didn't care. I just wanted to get that off my chest. I'd been trying to be a better person. I knew I had done some dirt in my life, and I had been thinking about giving myself to the Lord. After that scare I had with Lance, maybe if I prayed and went to church at least one Sunday out of the month, God would get that devil out of my life for good. I hoped he was done harassing me.

"Well, I'm glad y'all can get past that bull from the past. We're family, and we need to stick together and keep the nonsense and drama out of our circle," Melody admonished. She was always trying to fix other folks' broken relationships, but she couldn't fix her own. I just nodded my head in agreement. I wanted to hurry up and finish my food so I could get back to my husband. We were newlyweds, and I didn't want to be away from him too long.

34

Sasha

I really wasn't in the mood to look at Asia, let alone speak to her fake-acting ass. I knew I shouldn't have agreed to go out and eat with Melody. I knew she would have something up her sleeve. She didn't tell me that Asia would be joining us. When she arrived, I almost got up from my seat and walked out. But I had decided to stay because my mouth was watering for the tasty and fulfilling steak burrito they served. I didn't say anything to her; I acted as if she wasn't even there. That trick was such a hypocrite. She mentioned that she was thinking about going to a Baptist church so that God could forgive her of her sins. She had better be careful that she doesn't get struck down when she walks through the doors of the church. She was so confused about life and her place in it. She didn't know what the hell she wanted to do.

Last year she talked about becoming a Muslim because Steve told her that he was reading the Quran while he was locked up and that she needed to try it out. Melody asked her what made her decide that she wanted to join a Baptist church. That fool said that she was touched after she watched Kanye West's *Jesus Walks* video on BET. She said she wanted to right her wrongs. I almost choked on my drink listening to her dumb ass.

She went on and on about how she was being a better mother and how she thought she needed to give thanks to

God for delivering her. That was another reason why she said she wanted to start going to church. That was something new to my ears because all Asia did was call her kids names and talk down to them. She would call them fat ass, bastards, and retarded right in their face. I didn't want kids, and I didn't even like being around them, but I wouldn't call them names to their face because I knew that would affect their self-esteem.

As I drove home from the restaurant, I thought about the talk my mother and I had yesterday. I couldn't believe she didn't remember that she had done those horrible things to me as a child. And I couldn't believe that a doctor had diagnosed her with a mental illness, and she wasn't getting treated for it. After she left my apartment, I googled schizophrenia and found out that it was a disorder in which people interpreted reality abnormally. It affected how a person thought, felt, and acted. It couldn't be cured, but treatment may help. In severe cases, patients could see or hear things that were definitely not real.

I read that some of the signs of the disorder were hearing or seeing something that wasn't there. The patients could experience constant feelings of being watched, and they would oftentimes increase in withdrawal from social situations. I also read that the disorder caused inappropriate or bizarre behavior and irrational angry and fearful responses to loved ones.

As I read, I looked to see if it was genetic and found that the article I was reading said schizophrenia had a strong hereditary component. I, being my mother's child, had a 10 percent chance of developing the disorder. When I read that, it sent chills up my spine. I didn't want to read any more. What if I was in that 10 percent? My head started to throb at that thought.

I lay my head down for a few minutes to see if that would help. My mind wandered back to my childhood when my mother would lock me in the closet and tell me that she did that because someone was watching us or spying on us and trying to kill me. Her situation was crazy, but how in the world was she able to live a normal life and not take any medication after I left home? She had told me that she didn't believe what the doctor had told her, so she just walked out of the hospital.

I decided to do a little more research, and as I scrolled down the page on my computer, I saw that delusions and hallucinations were disturbances that were added to the person's personality. My mother was definitely delusional and paranoid; she always thought people were after us. She also would hear voices.

After I read all the information that I found on the Internet, I went to YouTube and watched interviews on people with the disorder. It brought tears to my eyes to hear what the people went through when dealing with issues in their everyday life. In the back of my mind, I thought that I should have someone talk to my mom to see what she can do to make her life better. But when we talked, she acted as if she hadn't had any symptoms.

She asked me why I hadn't told anyone that she did those things to me when I was young. I told her that I was scared to talk because I thought I would be taken from her and put in foster care. She understood where I was coming from. Then she dropped the subject and walked away like we weren't talking.

I wanted to spend more time with her, just to see how she acted throughout her everyday life. I told her that I forgave her for treating me the way she did because she didn't mean to do it; she was ill. It was crazy because we hadn't seen each other in years, and I carried so much anger around toward her. Now, I just wanted my mother back. I told her she could stay with me for a while.

She looked at me as if I were a ghost. Then she told me no. She said she wanted to be in the comfort of her own home. I didn't know what it was, but I was really worried about her, and I wanted to be there for her.

35

Melody

It was late at night when my doorbell rang. Immediately, I knew who it was, and as pissed as I was at him for standing me up the last time, I decided that I would let him in. I quickly threw on an oversized shirt and my extrathick robe to keep him from seeing my size and opened the door to let him in.

"You missed me?" He asked that question as if everything between us was okay.

"No," I said, but I was lying. Of course I missed him.

"You gon' turn on a light in this piece and let me see that pretty face of yours?" he questioned as he stepped inside and closed and locked the door behind him.

"Boy, it's almost midnight, and I'm half asleep. I ain't trying to turn on no lights and wake myself all the way up. What the heck do you want?" I snapped at him.

He was looking so good standing there that I was immediately wet for him.

"I want to talk," he said as he stepped around me and gave me that smile that made me fall in love with him.

"Mmm-hmm. That means you want to have sex with me. But the answer is no." I spoke with anger in my voice. Rodney didn't seem to hear me as he gently gripped my shoulders and spun me around until my back was to the door he had just stepped through.

"Come on, bae," he said as he stepped closer to me, forcing me to step back until my behind hit the door. "Trust me, I really do want to talk."

"No, Rodney, you want to fuck." I squinted my eyes angrily at him.

"I promise you I want to talk." He spoke sincerely.

"Okay," I said, still not believing him.

"I missed this," he said as he quickly slipped his hand inside of my robe and under my shirt, his fingers aiming straight for my sweet spot. "Don't you miss me too?"

Before I could help myself, my body reacted to him. "Yes." The word eased out of my mouth as my head fell back against the door.

It was almost like my body was starving for him. Quickly, I thrust my hips forward, trying to get everything his hand could offer me. I was so pissed with myself for giving into him in less than two minutes, but I would have to deal with that anger later. At that moment, Rodney was making me feel too good to focus on being mad at him.

"Good answer," he said as he lowered himself to his knees. The next thing I knew, he had his face in my sex chamber and had his tongue performing amazing tricks. My knees began to shake. I didn't know how much longer I would be able to stay on my feet. "Tell me you miss it," he said as he licked me so good tears began to fall from the corners of my eyes. I really missed him and told him so.

"I missed you." I spoke the truth.

"And I'm sorry for standing you up the other night," he responded.

Just when I was about to erupt all over his face, Rodney surprised me by quickly standing, lifting one of my legs, and thrusting inside of me so hard that I came immediately. "You know you're my boo, right?" He asked the question, but I was too far gone to give him an answer.

"You're my baby," he said as he screwed me so good that I thought I was going to die when it was all over. "You know I want you, Melody. I don't want nobody but you," he said. His words were exactly what I wanted to hear, had been waiting to hear. "And I promise you, I'm going to make things right," he whispered sexily in my ear. "Can I make everything up to you?" he asked. Because I couldn't talk, I just nodded my head up and down. "Good, bae, because I promise you I'm going to make it up to you. I'm going to treat you right." He panted in my ear as he thrust harder and harder.

That was it. As soon as I heard him say that, I exploded all over his thick shaft. "Yeah, baby, cum on this dick," he said as my juices waxed his pole. "Just like that," he said as I felt him filling me with nourishment for the baby that I was carrying for him—the baby he still didn't know about.

"You gon' let me make us right?" he asked that as the last of him filled me.

"Yes," I spoke breathlessly, more in love with him than ever.

"Good," he said as I felt him soften, and then slip out of me. "Now, I'm done talking," he stepped back, pulled my shirt back down, and closed my robe. "I'm sorry I didn't use a condom, but I missed you so much, I just had to get some of that. But you know how to take that pill, so we're good," he said as I heard him adjusting his clothes in the still dark room.

"Mmm-hmm," was all I said. It was much too late for any pills. His seed was already growing in me. And it was time for me to tell him that.

"Babe, I need to—" He cut me off before I could really get started.

"I gotta go, but I'ma be in touch. We gotta talk and see how we gon' put this thing back together again, okay?"

He spoke as he reached for the door, opened it, and stepped out. Then, he turned to me. "Sorry for waking you up." He winked moments before he walked away.

The next day, Asia and I decided to go on a shopping date. I decided not to tell her what happened with me and Rodney the night before. I didn't want anyone judging me for having sex with him again. I would just wait until we were all right; then I would tell them.

There was a grand opening at a boutique on Collingwood Avenue. Asia said that the guy that owned the joint was really cool, and he had nice T-shirts that he designed for women, men, and children. She said that they also had handmade jewelry, so I was geeked up to check the spot out because I loved unique jewelry, and I loved spending my money on one-of-a-kind pieces. If I found a few pieces that I liked, I would make a deal with the owner and do a photo shoot of a few women modeling the jewelry and shirts. That would put his name out there so people would visit his store and my name out there as the photographer.

My business was really booming. I was picking up a lot of clients, and they loved my work. Last week, I was honored to take photos for this gorgeous wedding party. The person that contacted me was at Asia's wedding, and they loved her pictures, so they had me capture the special moments at their own wedding.

I was still looking for a building to expand my business. I was not going to just pick the first thing I saw. It was becoming frustrating at times. I would think that I had found the perfect spot, but then something would backfire. Most of the people I came in contact with that were leasing buildings were only in it for the money. They didn't care to try to meet the leaser halfway, maybe because I was a woman and they thought that they could run game on me. I was getting tired of the craziness.

A few months back, I had given the guy the deposit amount that he asked for, but he gave it back to me because someone else was willing to pay more than the asking price. I was looking for something special, and I wasn't going to stop until I found what I wanted. And, I didn't want a prick for a landlord. They better not mess with me because I would sue at the drop of a dime.

We entered the boutique, and the place was amazing. The lighting was glistening from the chandelier that hung low from the ceiling. The colorful and vivacious artwork on the wall really brightened up the establishment. The shirts and jewelry were one of a kind, and I was definitely going to talk to him about doing business with him.

After talking to him about my proposition, he told me he was down and that we could chop it up in a few weeks. I purchased two shirts and a few jewelry sets. Asia had a shopping bag full of goodies also. As we were about to exit the boutique, I saw Peaches walking through the door.

"What it do, boo?" Peaches smiled graciously and gave me a friendly hug.

"Hey, Peaches, what's up?" I returned the love. Peaches was a friend from the neighborhood that I grew up in. We were tight back in the day, but after we grew up, we went our separate ways. She said what's up to Asia and then continued her conversation with me.

"Girl, same shit, different toilet."

She giggled as she playfully hit me on my shoulder. "I know what you mean. I'm just trying to stay out of the way." I held my bag up to my stomach; I didn't want to reveal my pudginess.

"So, how is your love life?" She shifted all of her weight to her right side.

"It's good. Why do you ask?" I gave her a curt smile.

"Girl, no reason." She paused, then said, "Well, I was just asking because I saw Rodney in the club after hours last night, and I was hoping that y'all weren't together because he was all up in this chick's ear. She looked like a thirsty thot, and I was just wondering if y'all were beefing or what because, at the end of the night, he left with her. I would have gotten up in his face and checked him because you know you're my girl. I don't want that Negro screwing you over because I know you've been good to him," she said, rolling her neck. That girl didn't take a breath. She wanted to make sure her gossiping rant was out there.

"Thanks for telling me. I don't mean to cut you off, but I've got to go," I said with a straight face. I tried to keep my emotions together as the blood drained from my face. My heart had broken into a million pieces. "I'll see you around," I said as I walked out of the store, and Asia followed behind me.

On the ride home, I was silent until Asia broke the silence. "Melody, I know what Peaches told you hurt you, but you've got to see that dude ain't gonna change. He is gonna be who he is no matter how hard you try to change him or want him to be the man you want him to be. Girl, you act as if his thang is made of gold. The boy is going on forty; he ain't no man because if he was, he wouldn't treat you this way." She let out a deep sigh.

As I drove, I tried to hold the tears back, but I couldn't. I didn't have the energy to speak on what Asia had just said. I didn't want to say anything anyway because she was right. I had no comeback line for that. That man just kept on fuckin' with my emotions. If he didn't want to be with me, why the fuck couldn't he just tell me that instead of telling me that he loved me every night? If he wanted to be with someone else, why did he keep telling me that he wanted me and only me? I was furious, and

I knew just what I was going to do. I was so tired of him and his lies.

If I couldn't have him, then no one could.

After I dropped Asia off at her home, I drove into my driveway and walked in to my empty home. Rayn was with her father for the weekend. I dropped my purse and shopping bag on the couch and poured me a glass of Evian. Sasha turned me on to it when we were on speaking terms. I didn't drink hard liquor, but I needed something to ease my mind because I was thinking of doin' some crazy shit. I pulled my cell phone out of my pocket and dialed Rodney's number. I paced the floor thinking about what I was going to say to him. The phone rang three times and then, "Hello."

A high-pitched voice on the other end spoke into the receiver, and I lost it.

"Where the fuck is Rodney at?" I snarled loudly in the phone.

"Who's this?" she asked.

"Got-dammit! Trick, don't worry about who I am. Put Rodney on the phone." I couldn't believe he let a chick answer his phone.

"Sorry, but he's busy right now. Can I take a message?" She giggled maliciously.

I hung up on her ignorant ass. I was done. I paced the floor, trying to figure out my next move. I wanted to kill his ass for putting me through that mess. I was carrying his child. I was in love with him. I kept taking his shit because, in the back of my mind, I thought he would change. He told me that he wanted me, that I was his boo, that he loved me. I screamed out loud until my throat was raw. I had evil thoughts playing through my mind. I wanted to kill that muthafucka, and that was what I was going to do. But how? How could I kill his manipulative, no-good, lying, selfish, inconsiderate ass and get away with it?

I couldn't stop pacing the floor as I punched my fist into my other hand. That was when an episode that I watched on *Fatal Attraction* took over my thoughts. *Fatal Attraction* was a show on TV1. It was something like *Unsolved Mysteries*, but it focused on black folks that committed crimes against their partner. The episode that flooded my thoughts was when a woman was fed up with her boyfriend's cheating. She made love to him, and then, in the middle of the night, she set his ass on fire. The only thing I needed to make sure of was that Rodney had his clothes on before I lit the match and allowed his body to burn to a crisp.

The FBI found out that the man was naked when he died, so they knew it was a crime of passion, and they locked his ex up. Did I have the balls to do something like that? Did I really want to kill Rodney? I shook my head at my crazy thoughts.

"I just wish he was here right now. I would bash his head into this mirror and sit back and watch him as he bled to death!" I screamed out loud as my veins popped out of my neck, and my sweat drenched my clothes. I hated him so much at that very moment and wished that he could feel the pain in my heart so he wouldn't dare try to scar me again. I now knew how Lorena Bobbitt felt. I was losing my mind, and he was the cause. If he would have only kept it real with me and told me what he really wanted, then I wouldn't have been contemplating his death.

36

Asia

I tried to hold my composure when gossiping no-shame-in-her-game Peaches told Melody that Rodney left the club with a chick. I wanted to tell Peaches to stop starting a mess. She acted like she didn't know that he and Melody weren't together. She did that shit on purpose. She and Melody were cool in the past, but they didn't hang like they used to. I would see Peaches hoeing around town with a different man on her hip. She was the around-the-way girl, and every dude in the city tapped that, even Rodney. As much as we told Melody to leave that trifling, good-for-nothing Negro alone, it seemed like she kept falling deeper and deeper in love with hm.

On the way home, she was quiet. I wondered if she was thinking about how she was going to confront him when she got home. She was gonna take him back, no matter what, because that was just what she did. I always thought about her daughter and if she saw what her mother was going through in her dysfunctional relationship. I hoped that she didn't follow in her mother's footsteps. I wasn't gonna sit there and say that I had the best relationships in my life, but I didn't bring them in my house. Yes, I had three baby daddies, but my kids were not in the middle, and I never brought the men around. Well, not until I had their baby. As I thought about my life, I realized that maybe I wasn't a good example and that I shouldn't compare myself with Melody because we both made dumb mistakes in life. But now, I could say that I was good. I got my man, and I was happy. I wasn't going anywhere; I was going to make it last forever.

My man was on my mind, so I decided to surprise him with a home cooked meal. I wasn't a natural cook; I wasn't born to cook for a man and make him fall in love with me from the scrumptious meals I made. I cooked enough to survive a little bit here and a little there, but tonight, I wanted to try something special and hope that everything went well. I decided to make broccoli and baked potatoes to go with it. The kids were not home, so I hoped my dinner was good so I could be his dessert later.

"Hey, baby. It smells good in here. I know you ain't frying chicken," Steve said as he walked in the kitchen with shock in his eyes. He looked scared out of his mind, like I might give him salmonella or something. "Yes, babe. I'm frying chicken," I smiled.

"Hold up. What did I do? The kids not home. We're all alone. Why are you trying to kill me?" he said with a straight face.

I walked over and slapped him playfully on his shoulder. "This dinner is going to be good. Trust me."

"That's what a lot of women say to their men right before they poison them. I know you be watching *Snapped*."

"Stop it and sit down so I can fix your plate," I laughed. After I fixed our plates, we ate and had small talk.

"Wow, babe. This is pretty good. I'm so proud of you," he sang.

"Oh, so you're Drake now?" I asked in reference to him singing one of the lyrics to his song. We both laughed out loud.

"You already know what I want for dessert." Steve licked his lips and looked at me seductively.

"Whatcha want, daddy?" I purred. I knew what his answer was going to be, but I wanted to hear him say it.

"I want to devour that sweet potato pie between yo' legs."

I looked into his dreamy eyes as his words made me moist. "Okay, then. What are you waiting for?"

"After you, my lady." He stood up and waited for me to walk in front of him. Then we headed to the bedroom.

"Aww, you are being so romantic tonight. What have I done to deserve this?" he said as he looked at the single red rose that I placed in the center of the bed.

"You deserve that and more. You are a great provider, and you are a fantastic husband and father." Yes, I made more money than Steve did, but he was determined to pay most of the bills, and he worked his ass off to have a successful business.

He walked over to me and kissed me on the lips. Then, he forced his tongue in my mouth passionately, and our tongues slow danced.

"Babe, hold on a second. Let me get into something sexier." I turned around and looked into my drawer where I picked out a white lace, two-piece lingerie set. Then, I hurried into the adjacent bathroom to change.

"I don't know why you're putting that on. I'ma take it right off." He pouted as if he was a toddler that couldn't get his way.

"I know, but let me do this," I yelled from the bathroom.

I walked out of the bathroom, and my husband looked me up and down before he said, "Damn, you sho' look amazing. You dropped them pounds, and look at you now, looking like a supermodel. Come here so I can get in that. I'm ready for ya." He panted like a dog in heat.

I walked over to him, grabbed his head, and kissed him like I hadn't seen him in years.

He then laid my body down on our Egyptian cotton sheets and used his tongue to lick my wet spot. The lingerie was snapped between my legs, so he used his teeth to unsnap it. Then, he flicked his tongue gently around my sugar basin, and I cried out his name a billion times.

"Babe, don't run from me now. I've been waiting all day to taste you," Steve said between slurps.

I tried to stay still, but he knew exactly what to do to please my middle. "Baby, you make me feel so good," I moaned as he continued to please me.

That was one thing that I liked; he never stopped until I was completely satisfied. After I exploded with ecstasy, I got on my knees and returned the favor. I slid his manhood into my warm and moist mouth, and I went to town. I slurped and sucked until my man erupted in my mouth.

"Got-damn, baby! You are a beast with that mouth. Ooh-wee, I'm *so* ready to slide into that juicy, wet middle of yours." He grinned like he was a little boy in the candy store.

I got on top of him because he loved it when I rode it. I positioned myself as if I was about to do a squat on top of him. I moaned softy as I slipped his long and erect shaft inside of me.

"Asia, I love it when you take control," he said as his eyes rolled behind his lids.

He gripped my ass, and I started bouncing up and down as we both moaned out loud from the erotic pleasure. He filled me, and I loved the way he felt inside of me. I rode him, and my full-sized breasts bounced in the air. Sweat streamed down my back. I moaned out his name, and I flung my head back. I was on the edge, about to come. Right before I was about to let go, I looked over in the direction of my patio glass door and became scared shitless.

"Oh, shit!" I gasped as I hopped off of Steve's erect penis and covered my body in the sheets. I didn't dare look back over at the sliding patio doors that led out to our balcony.

"Baby, what's the matter? Did I hurt you?" Steve cried out. He tried to look into my eyes, but I avoided eye contact because I didn't want him to see the fear in my eyes. My heart was beating a mile a minute, and my whole body trembled as if I were in a freezer. I griped the sheet tight in my hands and held it up to my chest. I couldn't control myself; I couldn't speak to answer my husband's questions. All I could do was wonder how the hell Lance got on my second-story balcony, and why in the world was he looking through my doors, watching my husband and I make love?

37

Sasha

As I sat at my desk and prepared to write my next novel, chills ran up my spine. I was happy that a major publishing company accepted my manuscript that I wrote a few months back. I knew my writing was the shit because I wrote from the heart. A lot of sex scenes that I wrote were sweaty and hot because I lived out those scenes. I gave Lamel a lot of credit because, if not for him, I would still be daydreaming about the kinky things that we did. When I was with my husband, I fantasized so much and wished that one day my time would come. But now, I can say I made it. I'm a published author, and my first novel would be released later this year. And I can't wait for people to see my work. I smiled as I thought about my books being on the shelves of bookstores around the world.

It was not easy being an author; it took a lot of hard work and dedication to finish a book. Sometimes I would get writer's block. I would sit at my computer and want to write at least one thousand words, but nothing would come out. But I couldn't stop writing because I had deadlines to make. Sometimes I wanted to give up because, in the back of my mind, I would have thoughts about people rejecting my work and giving me bad reviews. I knew that everyone was not going to like my work, so I had to look past all the negative thoughts and think positively. I needed to write two books a year, so I decided to start on my second manuscript to get it out of the way. And what was so great about starting now was that my memory was still fresh from the night before when Lamel and I had the best sex ever. As I wrote the sex scene, our night replayed in my head.

I walked out to the bedroom from the bathroom wearing my lacy red, two-piece, see-through skintight lingerie. I reached for the light switch to turn the light off, and Lamel stopped me in my tracks and said, "Hell no. Leave them lights on; I want to see every move you make in that shit you got on. Damn, babe, you've got me rock hard. I don't even need no foreplay. Just come and jump on this." He licked his lips and cuffed his manhood in his hands. He was still fully clothed. "I'm just playing." He smiled seductively and continued. "I want to see you walk in those heels and that getup you've got on. Wait a minute; let's do something a little different. I want you to dance for me."

Lamel got up from the bed and walked over to the radio and pushed the button. Chris Brown's voice bellowed out. "There's something in this liquor, girl. I'm looking at your figure. I just want to see you strip right now." Those words did something to me. I started to grind my hips as I looked Lamel in his eyes. He couldn't keep his eyes off of my hips. I walked closer to him and started winding my hips closer to his body as he sat on the edge of the bed. I twerked a little. Then I turned around, and my backside faced him. I popped my ass on him, and as I gave him a lap dance a few minutes later, he slid his finger under my lingerie and into my wetness.

I moaned out loud, but I kept dancing as he pleased me erotically. He went deeper, and I gyrated slower.

I couldn't take anymore. I didn't have a teenage body any longer; I was hitting thirty-five, and my knees were getting weak. That dude made me young again, but I couldn't hang every night. I pushed myself up in a full stand, turned around, and kissed him hard as he gripped my ass, and then ripped the thin material off my body. My blood rushed through my body from pure lust because I knew what was about to go down. I snatched his shirt off over his head, unzipped his jeans, and filled my mouth with all of him, and he growled. A few minutes later, he lifted me up by my waist and laid me on my back. He slid himself inside of my warmness, and he stroked my insides long and hard. I screamed out in ecstasy until we both exploded.

My phone brought me back to reality. I put the pen down that I was writing with and picked up my cell phone.

"What are you doing?" Lamel's deep voice penetrated the line.

"Writing." My lips formed into a smile from the sound of his voice.

"Well, I hope it's real juicy, and I hope that I was an inspiration for that piece of work that you're creating."

I sucked my teeth. "You know you are."

"Was I beating that thang up? You better have had me in there, ripping yo' walls out," he said seriously.

I giggled.

"Well, I don't want to stop you from focusing on what you do. But I wanted to ask you if you wanted to go to this, um, this sex party."

My eyes bulged out of my head. "Sex party?"

"Yes, it's a co-ed party, and we all dress up in costumes, you know; a sexy costume, and we just show up. It's going to be a lot of stuff going on, and I don't want to tell you everything because I want you to see for yourself."

"What, you've been to one before?" I wanted to know. But from the way he was talking, I already knew the answer.

"Yes, I went to one a few years back. You know I'm a party animal; there isn't a party that I haven't been to. This is different, though, and I think you'll like it."

"Okay, I'll go," I said without putting much thought into it. Everything we did was spontaneous, and I loved it.

"Good. I'll pick you up in about an hour."

"Wait . . . What am I gonna wear?" I said in a panic. I wouldn't be ready in an hour.

"Don't worry about that. I've got you. I'll be there shortly," he said right before he hung up.

That's what I enjoyed most about Lamel; he opened my eyes to new things. People that lived here, including myself, would say that Toledo was a boring place to live, but he would always find something to get into. Shoot, I enjoyed going to the strip club with him, somewhere I never thought I would go with a man.

Lamel finally arrived, and I was couldn't wait to see what he had brought me to wear.

"Hey, bae. I've got something sexy in here for you to wear. Get dressed so we can go," he said after kissing me with his full lips and handing me a plastic shopping bag.

I grabbed the bag and took the piece of lace fabric out of it. Then I opened up the bag wider to see where the rest of the outfit was. "What is *this*?" I said with an attitude as I held what looked like a black, lace shoestring. I knew he didn't think I was going to wear that. I would look like a cheap hooker.

"Why you acting like that?" he smiled. I didn't see nothing funny. "I went to this sexy lingerie store in the mall, and I looked hard to find something that will have you looking like no other. You will be the baddest chick at the party. I think you'll like it better when you put it on. Bae, sometimes you gotta think out of the box."

"No, I'm going to find a box to put this in." I looked at the fabric again. "This thing won't cover up one of my breasts," I shrieked.

"Calm down; it stretches," he said as if he solved the problem. Then, he continued. "Just go and try it on, and let me be the judge of how it looks."

I shook my head and walked into the bedroom. I didn't want to look like a fool and put it on in front of him because I knew it wasn't going to work out. After I struggled to stuff my size ten frame into what looked like a size two onesie, I was shocked at the result. The one-piece lingerie fit my curves nicely, and the material also pushed up my breasts and lifted my butt. I liked it, but it was something I wouldn't wear out at a club. This was bedroom wear only. I walked out of the bathroom and back to the bedroom. And when I looked at Lamel, his eyes looked as if they were about to pop out of their sockets.

"Daaaamn, you look phat!" He took my hand and turned me around to see my backside. Then he slapped me across my butt, and I jumped because I wasn't expecting that. "I can't wait to get you there. The men are gonna hate that I've got the sexiest and the baddest chick in the club." He smiled hard as he rubbed his hands together.

"I ain't wearing this out to no club. I don't have any clothes on. I look like a prostitute on the stroll. You're tripping," I spat.

"Babe, you look good for the occasion. This is what is worn at these types of parties. Please just come and you'll see. You will have the best time of your life. I promise you will enjoy yourself. Just trust me; I've got you." Lamel pleaded with me with his eyes. I was so caught up with what he got me that I didn't even notice that he was dressed in his costume. He had on some nice, form-fitting jeans, with a thick, black, leather belt, and black cowboy boots and hat. He had on a black bow tie around his neck without a shirt on. I told myself that I would try it, just once, and if I didn't like it, Lamel wouldn't hear the last of it. I would let him have it, and I guarantee he'd would have to make it up to me later. I got my stilettoes, and we headed out the door to the sex party.

38

Melody

"Rodney, why the hell have you been dodging me?" I yelled at him after I opened the door. He walked in and said, "I'm sorry, Mel. I've been tryin' to make this money. I had some stuff that I needed to take care of."

"Why didn't you come by the other day like you said you were? I was waiting up for you, and you never showed," I whined. As much as I hated how he treated me, I always got weak. As soon as I saw his face, the anger I had was no longer an issue.

"Um . . . I was gambling, boo, and when I got done, it was four in the morning. I knew you were in bed asleep. You know how it be when I'm trying to get that paper." He let out a deep sigh as if he had a bad night. He played cards and pool for money.

"Gambling never stopped you from coming over to my house at four at the morning no other time," I spat. I wasn't going to let him get away with his lies that easily.

His eyes shifted from my face to my belly bump. I was wearing a shirt that was snug against my upper body. "Melody, are you pregnant?" he asked with wide eyes.

I took my right hand, rubbed my stomach, and gave him a half smile, "Yes." I couldn't tell by his blank expression what he would say next.

There was a brief pause; then he said, "Last time I came in you, I told you to get that pill." He squinted his eyes and gave me a look that said he was confused.

"I know, but, um . . . that day . . . I had become so busy and I . . . I kind of forgot. And when I remembered, it was like . . . um, three days later," I lied. I couldn't look him in his eyes. I never planned on getting that morning-after abortion pill. I wanted his baby because I knew that would make us become closer in our relationship.

"Damn, Melody." He walked over and flopped down on the couch. I knew he was going to be mad, but I hoped he would get over it.

"Rodney, I'm sorry, bu—"

"Melody, you should be sorry." He cut me off as he got up and walked toward me. "How far along are you?" He looked at my stomach again.

"I'm about four months," I stuttered. I knew he wasn't about to tell me to have an abortion because that was not happening.

"Why didn't you tell me sooner? You've been around here with my seed, and you didn't even tell me. I should have been here for you while you were going through morning sickness and your late-night food cravings." He was angry, but his tone was soft.

"You're not mad at me for not taking the pill?" I looked into his eyes.

"I'm mad because you kept this from me. I shouldn't have told you to get that pill. I love you, and it takes two to tango." He got on bended knee to rub my stomach. I smiled at his corny words, but my heart warmed when he caressed me in his arms.

My cell phone ringing woke me up from my dream. I sat up in bed and picked up the phone from my nightstand. "Who's this?" I said to myself after I looked at the number and didn't have a clue who it was.

I cleared my throat. "Hello."

"Hi, is this Melody?" a female's voice on the other end said.

"Who is this?" I recognized the voice but couldn't picture her face.

"This is Tasha, Rodney's sister."

"Oh, how you doing?" I forgot to save her number in my phone when we bumped into each other at the beauty shop. She must've been calling to set up a date for us to get a bite to eat.

"Not too good. Rodney is in the hospital in serious condition; he got shot last night." She now had sorrow in her voice.

"What!" I shouted. There was a brief pause. My heart dropped to my stomach. I jumped from my bed and paced the floor. Words wanted to come from my mouth, but they were stuck in my throat.

After telling myself to breathe, I asked, "Is he going to be okay? Can I see him?" Tears fell from my eyes because when she said he was in serious condition that didn't sound good at all.

"Yes, he's in Toledo Hospital, room 342."

I sat on the edge of my bed so I could calm down. It felt as if my legs were about to give in. "I'm on my way now." I got off the phone, threw on a pair of sweatpants and a wrinkled, loose-fitted tee shirt, got my keys, and I was out of the house in no time.

Walking into Rodney's room was the worst thing I had ever experienced. Instantly, I felt sick to my stomach, and without realizing it, I reached out my hand and began to rub my belly and the baby within. It was hard for me, watching him lying in that bed, tubes attached to his body that were connected to all kinds of machines. He looked as if he would die at any minute. I couldn't help the tears that fell from my eyes. The strong, sexy man that I loved was nowhere present, and in his place was a person that looked weak and frail and standing at death's door. I was terrified, my anger toward him instantly forgotten.

Struggling to accept what I was seeing, I was in shock. I wanted so badly for this to not be true, but it was, and I needed to face it. His eyes were closed as I walked up to his bed and placed my hand over his. His sister was sitting on the other side of the bed, looking as sad as I felt, but she looked worried as well because her brother was still in danger.

Rodney was only allowed two people in his room at one time. If your name wasn't on the list at the nurse's station, then you couldn't enter his room or call him. Security was on high alert since they were still looking for the guy that shot him, and everyone was on the lookout in case the guy showed up at the hospital to finish the job.

When I was finally able to control my emotions, I asked Tasha what happened.

"Girl, some fool shot him in the chest at the club. The people on the scene said the dude was mad because Rodney was dancing with his girl. But some other people said that the dude and Rodney had beef in the past, and he came in there looking for Rodney. Apparently, they had some words, and that's when the dude pulled out his gun and shot him." She paused to catch her breath. She was emotional and hurt at the fact that her brother was lying unresponsive in the hospital bed. I understood exactly how she felt. I didn't know what to say, so I just held his hand and looked at his face. I was glad that Tasha had called me. It didn't matter what we had been through; I loved that man with all my being, and I was going to be there for him, no matter what.

"My brother has a collapsed lung, and his intestines and a few of his other organs are all screwed up from that traveling bullet. The cops haven't found who did this shit to him yet, and if they don't find him soon, *I'm* going to have to get involved," Tasha announced. I was surprised at her words, especially since she didn't seem to have the tough guy personality. I felt her, though. When it came to family, you were down for anything to make sure justice was served.

I stayed at the hospital the entire first week that Rodney was in there. The whole time I was praying for him to wake up. Around day number four, he did just that. The moment I saw him moving, the tears started to fall from my eyes, and nurses rushed into the room. That's when he opened his own eyes and looked at me.

"Why are you crying?" he questioned me as the nurse stood there taking his vitals and administering medicine through one of his tubes.

"Because you're hurt," was my quiet response.

"I'll be all right. It's just a gunshot." He tried to joke, but I found nothing funny. "You remember being shot?" the nurse questioned.

"Unfortunately, yeah," he said as he coughed a little. That made me cry some more. "Come on, Mel." His speech began to slur. "Everything is going to be all right."

Before I could give him any type of response, his eyes began to close, and the next thing I knew, he was snoring lightly.

"This kind of medication kicks in really fast. I had to give it to him to ease the tremendous pain he's going to be in. He'll be out for a while; then, when he wakes, the police will be here to take his statement, so you may as well go home and get some rest." I took the nurse's advice, but I was back every day. I was there when he woke up, talking to him, and making sure he was doing okay. That went on until his eighth day there. That was when I finally decided to tell him about the baby.

"I'm pregnant," I said to him after I had heard the nurses telling his sister that although he had organ issues, he was doing much better than everyone expected. "What?" he asked, looking at me like I was crazy.

"I'm pregnant," I repeated myself.

That's when he looked me up and down, and in his eyes, I could see things falling into place. "That's why you've been gaining weight," he reasoned to himself. Then, he paused for a moment, as if in thought, and said, "You didn't take that pill, did you?"

"No." I was honest.

"Which time?" He wanted to know.

"The time before the last one."

"So, when I came to your house last week, you were already pregnant?"

"Yes."

He was doing it again, being quiet. But that didn't last long because, before I knew it, he went off. "You took my money but didn't take the pill! You trapped me, Mel! You trapped me into having a baby! You *know* I don't want any more kids, so you trapped me."

"I didn't trap you," I tried to defend myself.

"Then why? Why didn't you get that pill?" He was so angry that the machines he was hooked up to started going haywire.

"Because I forgot," I lied. "I woke up the next day, and a lot of stuff happened. I was busy for a few days, and by the time I remembered, it was too late to take the pill." I knew he wouldn't believe me, but it was all I could come up with.

"You're crazy, and you're trying to trap me!" He was adamant about that, but I was cool with his attitude because, in all of the fussing he was doing, he never once told me that he wanted me to get an abortion. So, I stood there and took his fussing, not really caring because, in the back of my mind, all I cared about was him getting healthy and the fact that we were going to be a family.

"Sir, you're going to have to calm down," the nurse said as soon as she stepped in, but Rodney kept right on fussing. The next thing I knew, she said it was meds time, and within minutes, his voice lightened, his speech slurred, and he was knocked out.

It was going on two weeks since Rodney had been in the hospital. "Hello, Miss Melody, you can go in now," the nurse said.

"Thank you," I said as immediately I got up from my seat and walked out of the waiting room and down the hall to Rodney's room. He was still in serious condition because his organs and lung were still healing, but he was doing much better.

"Hey, babe. How are you feeling?" I smiled and kissed him since he was sitting up in bed.

"I'll be good when I can go to the bathroom by myself," he huffed. He had a catheter in, and I could tell he was uncomfortable.

"How are you feeling about our conversation?"

He pouted in response to my question. I knew he was still mad at me for finally telling him I was pregnant a few days ago. He'd been upset then, and from the looks of things, he was upset now. But I wouldn't argue—not only for the baby's sake, but for his sake as well. Although he wasn't acting like it, especially since he'd just gotten out of bed and was walking around, Rodney was a very sick man.

"Now, Rodney, you need to stop walking around; stay off your feet and rest your body. You don't want to hurt yourself and have to start all over again with your healing," the nurse said calmly and gave him a stern look right before she walked out the door.

"I don't have time to be sitting around. I need to get out here. I hate hospitals." He growled with anger as he paced the floor.

"Babe, if you do what they say, then you *can* get out of here," I tried to reassure him. I didn't understand why in the world he wanted to walk around anyways. He had to walk with a walker while holding on to the rack that held his urine and IV.

"I'm going to be cool; they just need to release me." He got back on his bed as if he was out of breath and closed his eyes.

I hoped he would keep still so he could get out of there, so we could get to being a family.

It had been a long week. After I left the hospital from seeing Rodney a few days ago, I rushed home to do a photo shoot. It went well, and my client really loved the pictures that I shot of her and her three children. She purchased the deluxe package, which consisted of five poses and four different backgrounds. That ran for $300. The client had referred me to two more of her friends, and they made appointments for the same week. One of the ladies was a model, and she needed a few shots to send to her agent because her other photos were ruined in a house fire. I really enjoyed her shoot because she knew how she wanted to pose, and she was a pro at it.

The other client that I had wanted me to take a few graduation photos of her daughter, Samantha, who was graduating from high school. Samantha was very shy, and I could tell she was not comfortable in her skin. I had to tell her over and over again that she was beautiful. She was a dark-skinned teen, weighing about two hundred sixty pounds. Her mother was in the background yelling at her to smile differently because the smile she was giving wasn't cute. I hated parents like that. The parents that didn't let their children be who they were. The kind of parents that constantly criticized their children and made them feel bad. I wanted to tell her to go outside while I did my job because I was getting sick of her, and Samantha definitely wasn't feeling it, which didn't help with the shoot.

On top of working, I also had to take Rayn to basketball practice three times a week. While she was there, I went home to cook dinner, and then rushed back to pick her up. I wasn't able to move like I used to with a baby in my stomach. I had finally told Rayn that I was pregnant. She was excited that she was going to have a baby brother or sister, but she was sad that Rodney had gotten shot. I assured her that he was going to be just fine.

I still had not told my mother, Asia, or Sasha. I had been so busy with everything that was going on in my life that I hadn't seen my cousins in a few weeks. When my mother called, we talked about everything else, so I never brought up the fact that I was pregnant. I knew that she would be upset because I wasn't married, so I really wasn't in a rush to tell her. I wasn't ready to hear her gripe about it.

I was supposed to go and see Rodney at the hospital, but I was just too tired. I talked to him on the phone the day before, and he sounded like he was out of breath. Maybe it was good that I didn't go and see him; it seemed like he needed his rest. I lay my head down on my pillow and was asleep within seconds. But my sleep was soon disrupted by the ringing of my phone.

"Ugh, who is this calling me at three in the morning?" I was irritated because I was sleeping so well. I picked the phone up and answered with an attitude. "Hello."

"Melody!"

"Yes," I said in a calm tone. It was Tasha.

I heard the tears in her voice when she said, "Rodney just passed away."

I shot up in bed like a bullet. "What did you say?"

"Rodney passed away!" Tasha wailed as if in great agony.

I inhaled deeply from shock, but I couldn't exhale. I went mute. It felt as if someone punched me in the stomach. All the wind in my body was snatched from within me. I could hear Tasha on the phone saying something, but I couldn't focus on her words. *Rodney can't be dead! I just talked to him yesterday!* My heart ached, and my head spun. My hands shook so badly that I couldn't hold on to the phone any longer. The device fell from my hands and landed on my bed.

"Noooooo!" I screamed until I was hoarse.

39

Asia

Ever since I saw Lance peeking into my bedroom through my balcony door, I had been watching my every move. I couldn't believe that he would do something so insane. After I saw him watching that night, I got up and ran to the bathroom. Chills ran up my spin. He was really looking through my fucking window. My body shook uncontrollably. I was so messed up that I needed to be by myself behind walls where there were no windows. I felt so violated as I wondered why in the hell Lance was doing that to me. My husband banged on the door, wanting to know what was wrong with me. But I didn't answer him. I just sat on the toilet and cried. I was too distraught to come up with a lie like I did at my wedding when I saw Lance.

He was getting out of control, and I had to do something about it. I had to tell my husband, and when he got home from work, that was what I was going to do. I sat in my home office, going through paperwork from the last couple of homes that I'd sold, but I couldn't concentrate. All I could do was go back to the time when Lance and I were together to see if I could remember any time that I thought he was the crazy, stalking type.

I put the paperwork down on my desk, sat back in my leather chair, and thought hard, but I couldn't come up with anything. Then I remembered the time I told him I was going out for Melody's birthday. I told him what club I was going to, and he didn't want me to go because he said there were too many thirsty dudes in that club, and that I shouldn't be in that crowd. I wasn't trying to hear what he was saying, so I went anyway.

I was chilling at the bar when I looked across the bar and saw who I thought was Lance staring at me. But when I got up to go confront him, he was no longer there. I couldn't understand why he would follow me to the club, just like I couldn't believe he would drive me off the road. Back then, I thought it was cute that he wanted to see what I was up to. I never thought he would be the type to try to kill me, then find out where I lived and peek through my window while my husband and I made love.

I shook my head to rid the thoughts that were flooding my mind. I looked at the time; it was after midnight, and my husband was not at home. I walked upstairs to make sure that the kids had turned the TVs off in their rooms before they went to bed. Joey had a bad habit of going to sleep with his TV on. I always had to get on him about that. I told him he needed to cut that out or get a job and help pay the electric bill.

I walked into each of my children's rooms and tucked them in. They were sleeping so peacefully. Looking at them brought Lance back into my mind, his words playing over in my head like a broken record. "*I will blow up your house with you and yo' kids in it.*"

I still didn't understand how he got my address. He must have followed me because my address was not listed. I did that because I was a Realtor, and I had come across a few crazy people looking for houses. A few had gotten mad because they didn't get the houses that they wanted, and I didn't want them to come looking for me. However, on that day, I wasn't worried about how an old client got my address. I was losing my mind because my ex-lover was stalking me.

After I took a hot shower to relax, I walked into my room to find my nightclothes. Before I put them on, I went back in the bathroom to get dressed. I was so scared that Lance was outside my door watching me. I wished Steve would get home. I wondered where in the hell he was at one in the morning.

When I finished getting dressed, I opened the bathroom door and heard my phone ringing. I picked it up quickly because I knew it had to be Steve.

"Where are you?"

"Oh, you're looking for me? I'm not too far, so I can pay you a visit if you want," the voice on the other end said and then let out a sinister laugh.

"Lance, you better not come back over to my house, or I will call the police," I spat. I looked over at my patio door to see if he was near.

"You little whore. I knew you had it in you, so why didn't you ever ride me like you were riding your husband? You were getting it like a champ," he said, and I went mute. I was about to hang up the phone, but he must have read my mind.

"If you hang up on me, I'll be over there in five minutes. Try me, bitch!" I sat down on the bed as one tear dropped from my eye.

"Now answer me, dammit. Why didn't you take control in the bed with me like you did with that lame husband of yours?"

"I have to go; my husband is coming in the room," I lied.

"You're a liar; I know your husband isn't there. And if you lie to me again, I *will* be knocking on your door before the whole lie comes outcha mouth." His voice was stern. I swallowed hard but didn't say a word.

"I know your husband is out, driving your car. By the way, I see you upgraded your ride after totaling your other car. I like it; it's nice."

That was it. I snapped. "No, I *didn't* total my car—*you* did!" I was enraged. "Why did you try to kill me? Why the hell are you stalking me, showing up at my home and at my wedding? What the fuck is *wrong* with you?" I shouted because I wanted to make sure he heard me clearly. I was beyond pissed; I was ready to find someone to do him in.

"Asia, if I can't have you, no one will. I loved you with my whole heart, and you went out and got married on me. Oh, babe, I'm not going *anywhere,* and one day, it will be *my* ring that you will wear on your finger. You need to stop fronting; you know you love me. What do you see in the dude you're with? He looks like he's a little fruity. Are you sure that he wasn't getting bent over while he was locked up." He laughed out loud.

"You sick bastard! No, my husband is *not* gay," I spat.

"Are you *sure?*" His laugh was sinister.

I couldn't help it; I hung up the phone. I just sat there, immobile, terrified that he would show up at my house again. I called Steve's phone, but it went straight to voice mail. My phone was ringing off the hook, but I refused to answer it. I didn't want to hear anything else Lance had to say. I was going to have to get a restraining order on him. I couldn't sleep, and I wondered where the hell my husband was.

Finally, the ringing began to drive me insane. I picked up my phone, pushed the talk botton, and shouted, "Stop calling my mutha—"

"Asia, it's me. Melody." I could hear in her voice that she was crying.

Ugh. I didn't want to hear about her and Rodney's issues. He had to have done something wrong because it was the middle of the night, and she was calling me. As soon as I realized it was her on the line, Steve walked through the door.

"Rodney's dead! I'm about to lose my mind! Can you please come over?"

"Are you kidding me? Oh my God! I'm on my way," I said and got up from the bed.

"What's wrong?" Steve came in, looking like he was concerned.

"My cousin needs me. I'll deal with you when I get back." I gave him a toxic glare. I walked out of the bedroom and out my front door without saying another word to him.

40

Sasha

I didn't know what to expect as I walked into the club half naked for the sex party. But once I entered the huge building, which looked like an old warehouse, my mouth literally dropped to the floor. There were men that walked around with thongs on with suspenders. Most of all the women had on bras and thongs, but some of them were decent, wearing one-piece lingerie or swimming suits with stilettoes. People gathered around talking, drinking, and smoking weed. When I looked up, there was couple on sex swings, hanging from the ceiling. I had never seen anything like that in my life.

As I looked to the left of the room, there was porn playing on a large screen. The screen was in the middle of a large wall, and there was a woman lying across the table with different types of food on her body for people to pick up and eat. I was not about to eat food off of a naked woman's body. I didn't care if her private parts were covered. That was disgusting.

As we walked farther down a narrow hall by the restrooms, I saw that there were also private rooms where the guests could go in and watch XXX movies with their mate and do whatever they pleased during the video. There was just sex everywhere, and I really wasn't feeling the visual that I was getting.

There were also large rooms where different types of music were being played, and the dance floor was packed with people sweating, moving their bodies seductively to the music, and just having a good ol' time. A few people were making out by the walls or on the leather sofas for all to see. I wasn't used to these types of events; I actually felt dirty and out of place. Men walked around gawking at me as they eyed me up and down. But when I looked at Lamel, it seemed as if he was having a good ol' time, and everywhere he went, he pulled me with him.

Lamel decided that he wanted to go inside the room, which was the size of a miniclub, to listen to rap music. We danced a few songs, and then, in the middle of the song, someone passed Lamel a joint. He hit it, and then asked me if I wanted to hit it. I hadn't smoked weed since I was in college. I didn't smoke often, only when I went to a few parties. However, weed did make me relax a little and not worry about the small things. Maybe that was what I needed at that moment because I was on the verge of telling Lamel I was ready to go. I took the joint from his hand and took a long drag. Instantly, I felt like I was hit in the head by a semitruck. But the feeling was not painful; it just knocked me off my feet. I felt Lamel grab me.

"Damn, babe, are you all right? You need to take yo' time when you hit that. This stuff ain't no regular shit you get from yo' homegirls," he smiled.

He wasn't lying. The stuff that I smoked back in the day didn't come close to what I had in my hand. I figured it was just the upgraded version, especially since it smelled different and tasted like no other weed I had had before. But the feeling it gave me was magnificent, and I kept smoking it until it was gone.

That's when I started dancing like I was a pro at it. I got close to Lamel, turned my back to him, pressed my ass into him, and started twerking like crazy. Up and down, I moved on him like I was giving him a standing lap dance. I could feel him getting hard as a rock as his manhood slipped between my cheeks through our clothes.

"Come on, baby, the way you're twerking on this dance floor has my man on fire. Let's go somewhere and handle this," he said as he grabbed his crotch.

I may have been high, but I was not about to have sex for all the public to see. "Lance, let's go home or to a hotel; I don't want to do it here." My eyes begged him.

"Babe, I can't drive like this, and you can't either. We need to let our high go down a little. I've got a place where we can get some privacy. Come on."

He took my hand and guided me. He had begun to look a little strange. What did he mean we couldn't drive? We were only smoking weed which was legal in some states. But I didn't say a word, I just followed behind him. On the way to our destination, someone passed another joint to him, but instead of him hitting it, he gave it right to me. I was going to refuse it, but I took it and hit it a few times. I needed to be ready for what was in store.

Lamel walked with me into the women's room. There were six stalls along with a counter that had six sinks and a large rectangular mirror that hung on the wall. He checked every stall to see if someone was in them. The restroom was empty, so he turned around, walked to the door, and turned the dead bolt to lock it.

"I can't wait; I need you right now." Suddenly, he pulled me close and kissed me violently.

He shoved his hands into my panties and began a rough massage of my clit. Instantly, I became weak in the knees, thrusting my private part toward his rewarding fingers. I was not only horny, I was high as hell. After he kissed me, Lamel swung my body over to where the mirror was. I was now facing it, and I placed both of my hands flat on it as he pulled his pants down, pulled my thong to the side, and rubbed his erect penis up and down my soaked slit.

I moaned, and that's when he pushed the head in, but only the head. I was on fire, pushing my ass on him, trying to get him inside of me. Quickly, I began to twerk on him again, and without warning, he plowed his erect penis inside of me. I inhaled deeply because the feeling was like no other. It felt like he ripped my insides apart from the force—but I liked it, and I screamed out loud like a crazed maniac.

"Sasha, lift yo' head up and look in the mirror," he said as he grabbed a handful of my hair and pulled it back so that I could look at him in the mirror as he pounded me from the back. The sight of us in that mirror with him ramming into me turned me on even more. I looked at him through the mirror as I slowly swirled my tongue around my lips, bouncing my ass on him the entire time. "Damn, your facial expressions are turning me on," he growled.

I bit my bottom lip and moaned with every hard stroke he delivered as my sweaty palms were pressed against the mirror. We were in some kind of weird, erotic, sexual zone. My heart was racing, pounding; I was screaming like crazy. I was on the verge of an epic explosion, and I could hear him getting close as well—Then there was a knock at the door. I tried to hold my screams in. I didn't want to stop, but whoever was at the door was pounding harder and harder and shouting, "Open the door! This is a multistall restroom. This door shouldn't be locked."

It seemed as if the chaos was turning him on even more because, with every pound on the door, Lamel banged harder inside of me. My middle was gushing wet; I was ready to burst. But I was sweating uncontrollably, and my mouth was suddenly really dry. I tried to tell

Lamel to stop so that I could catch my breath, so that I could breathe, but I couldn't get my words out as I tried to balance myself on the mirror. It felt as if I were on a roller-coaster ride and was losing control of my balance and my vision at the same time. Then, all of a sudden, everything went black.

When I woke up, I was in a hotel bed, confused about what had happened the night before. My head throbbed, and my insides ached. It felt like someone had shoved a pole between my legs.

I knew I hadn't been raped. Or had I? I looked over at Lamel. He was still asleep. I then focused on the neon-colored numbers on the digital clock that was on the nightstand next to me. It was after one o'clock. I wanted to lie back down from the pain in my head, but I needed answers.

"Lamel, wake up," I shouted.

"What's wrong?" He jumped up and wiped the sleep from his eyes.

"What happened to me last night?" I looked deep into his eyes.

He squinted and said, "You're waking me up out of my sleep to ask me that dumb-ass question?" I was alarmed because he never cursed at me before.

"Yes. I need to know, and I need to know now!" I spat with anger. "All I remember is going to a sex party that was packed with over five hundred people, all the rooms, and smoking a lot of weed. Now, I'm in this hotel room, and I don't remember getting here," I blurted out.

"Yeah, we were both fucked up. You passed out when I was hitting that thang from the back," he said and slapped me on the ass. Then, he continued. "After that, I picked you up, drove us to the nearest hotel, and here we are. Oh, and that shit you were smoking wasn't just weed. We were coco-puffing," he said and lay back down.

My heart stopped. "What the fuck did you just say?" He was silent. "Did you just say that I was smoking weed laced with crack cocaine?"

"Yes, we were." His words were short.

"You bastard! Why would you do that? Why would you give me that shit to smoke?"

"What are you talking about? You're a grown-ass woman. I thought you knew what you were getting yourself into," he said, not looking at me. His head was turned as he lay on his pillow. "You know I don't do drugs." My blood was boiling. I couldn't believe what I was hearing. I couldn't believe that I was smoking crack and fucking at a party. And I didn't know what else went down because I couldn't remember. I didn't know who Lamel was anymore, and I was ready to choke the life out of him. He seemed to not even care that I was so distraught. He actually thought it was cool to give me that shit without telling me what was in it. I shoved him on his back with all of my might and said, "Get the fuck up and take me home—now!"

41

Melody

"Melody, I'm so sorry to hear about Rodney." Asia held me in her arms, trying to comfort me as we sat on the sofa in my living room. The shirt she was wearing was wet from my tears. As much as I tried, I couldn't stop crying. It was the middle of the morning when I called Asia; I didn't think she would answer. But she did, and she rushed right over to be by my side. I was a mess, and I still couldn't fathom what was going on.

"I had just talked to Rodney the other day, and he was walking around and doing fine," I cried as I wiped my nose with the tissue she gave me.

"I know you told me that he was recovering. So what went wrong?"

"His sister called me and told me that he'd caught pneumonia. That was what caused his death."

"Wow, that's horrible."

"I told him to stop walking around, and look at what happened; he got fluid in his lungs. He was just so hardheaded; now he's gone. I have no one to help me raise my baby," I cried some more. My body shook, and I was beginning to feel hot.

"Baby? You're pregnant?" Asia looked at me with wide eyes.

I nodded my head.

"Oh, Mel, I'm so sorry." She hugged me tighter.

I felt like disappearing; I wanted the nightmare to go away. Why did this have to happen to me? Why was my life so fucked up? I hated the way that I felt. It seemed as if I would never get over the feelings that I was experiencing at that moment. "This is all my fault," I whined.

"Why would you say something like that?" Asia wanted to know. She looked deep into my eyes as if she was looking for an answer there.

"I was so angry with him after I heard he'd left the club with some chick the other night. When I called his phone to confront him, a woman answered." I shook my head, not wanting to revisit that painful moment. "After I hung up the phone, I contemplated killing him."

"What!"

I paused at the shock in Asia's voice; then I continued. "I loved him with all my heart, and I was so upset that I wanted to kill him. I thought about so many different ways to make him suffer. Now look. Now, he's really dead. Oh my God! I really didn't want him to die." I cried until my voice went hoarse.

"Mel, you need to calm down. You are going to upset the baby. It was not your fault. Rodney was at the wrong place at the wrong time. I need you to breathe. Do you hear me?"

I didn't answer her; I just stared into space. "Rodney can't be dead!" I was hysterical, desperate for his death to not be real. "Take me to the hospital; I want to talk to him. I want to see him!" I got up to find my shoes.

"Mel, Rodney's gone. He's in a better place." Asia took my hands and held them tightly in front of me. I guess she thought that would stop me from trying to go to the hospital.

"Are you going to take me, or do I need to drive?"

"You are not going anywhere. How about I lie down with you, and in the morning, we can call his sister and see if there is something you can do for them to help with anything?" Her voice was calm.

"Who's gonna help me? I just lost the love of my life. I would bend over backward for that man. Who gonna see me through this sorrow in *my* life?" I shouted.

"I'm here for you. Don't you see that? You don't have to go through this alone."

"Oh my God! Rodney's dead; Rodney is really gone." I sobbed with my head in Asia's lap until I fell asleep.

I was on my way to the beauty shop; the last few days had been a living hell. I was trying my best to stay strong for Rayn and the baby inside of me. Today was the day I would see Rodney for the last time. His homegoing was at noon. I called my beautician to get me in on Friday, but she was booked. She told me that she could squeeze me in at nine on Saturday, the morning of the funeral. I hoped that she would work her magic because I still had to go home and get dressed. I laid my black, short sleeved, knee-length dress out on my bed so I could just slip it on and head to the church after my hair appointment.

When I walked into the shop, I sighed deeply. It was packed. But I couldn't tell who all was waiting on my beautician because there were other women doing hair in the shop. I waved at her to let her know I was there, and she told me that she would be right with me. I sat in the lobby and waited. I was happy to hear her voice within twenty minutes of me waiting. "Hey, Mel," she said and gave me a hug. "I'm so sorry about your loss. You're in my prayers."

"Thanks," was all I said because I knew that if I would've said more, the tears would've overcome me.

"Come on back to my seat so I can put your relaxer in."
   She relaxed my hair and tried to have small talk, but I really wasn't in the mood. I just wanted the day to be over with. There were a few other women in the shop talking about how sad it was that Rodney got shot in the club and how the police still hadn't found who shot him. I didn't say a word; I just ear hustled. I was so weak. I couldn't remember when the last time I had eaten. I rubbed my stomach, feeling sorry for my baby because I knew I was not taking care of my body like I should've been. To tell the truth, I really didn't care. I didn't want to be in my life at this point. But I knew I had to keep going for Rayn.
   Time was ticking, and it was getting closer and closer to the time when the funeral would start. I was under the dryer. It had taken her a little longer than I thought to relax my hair. She had to keep stopping because there were children in her shop that were acting up. I wished that parents wouldn't just drop their damn kids off. If I were a beautician, I would make their parents stay and wait while they were getting serviced. She was not a babysitter, and the kids were interfering with her other clients. I needed to get out of there, and I was becoming very irritated.
   I was pissed; I didn't get out of the shop until eleven forty-five. I sped to my house to get dressed, and then sped straight to the church. I knew I was going to be late, but I wasn't going to miss it for anything. When I got there, I wanted to look at him one last time and touch his hand and tell him that I loved him. The church was packed. I had to sit in the back. I began to weep uncontrollably when I saw that they had just closed the casket. Why the hell did they do that? They were not supposed to close the casket until the end of the funeral. I couldn't tell him I loved him. I couldn't even say good-bye. I wouldn't be able to see my baby's father ever again.

All the way to the cemetery, I cried my eyes out. I tried to control my tears because I didn't want to get into an accident due to my blurry vision. As I watched them lower him into the ground, my head spun, my knees went weak, and I fell to the ground. People I didn't even know rushed to my rescue. I felt so bad because I didn't want to take away from his service. I tried my best to keep it together, but I just couldn't.

An older lady with an oversized, fashionable hat came to me and gave me a bottle of water. "Here, drink this. You feel kinda warm. You might have a temp, sweetie." Her voice was sweet. I could tell she was concerned. When two men lifted me up from the ground, that same lady with the oversized hat gasped and said, "Oh, Lawd, you're pregnant! You need to see a doctor. I'm pretty sure you may have a temp, child."

"I'll be fine," I reassured her. But I knew what I said wasn't true. I wasn't fine, and I didn't think I would ever be fine. Tasha walked over to me, took my hand, and we walked away from the crowd. "Girl, I didn't know you were pregnant. Is it Rodney's?"

"Yes," I said with my head low. It was crazy that no one knew I was carrying his baby, but it was all my fault because I was the one who kept it a secret.

"Rodney and I were . . . Well, I was upset with him because I kept on hearing that he was cheating on me. So, I didn't tell him that I was pregnant until he was in the hospital. I tried to keep my distance from him because I was angry at the way he was always lying to me," I said, trying to explain the sad situation I was in.

"Girl, I told you that he was a ladies' man, and he loved you, but he wasn't ready to settle down."

Her words brought tears to my eyes. Even though she had told me that in the past, it still made my heart skip a beat.

"I'm hurting so bad because my baby will never get to meet its father." I covered my face with my hands and sobbed. My emotions were a wreck, and I knew it had to be my hormones also. Then I heard a voice, and I uncovered my face to see Rodney's mother standing right in front of me. I knew it was her because of a picture that I had seen on the wall at Rodney's house. "Are you going to be okay, child?" she asked in an irritated voice.

"Yes, ma'am. I'm sorry; I will be okay," I said as I cleared the snot from my nose.

"Ma, this is Melody, Rodney's girlfriend . . . She's pregnant," Tasha confessed.

I was mute as I looked at her eyes widen. "Pregnant? How come *I* didn't know about this before now?" She placed her hands on her hips.

I introduced myself to her, and I told her the same thing that I had just told Tasha, but Ms. Roberts wasn't having it. "Why haven't I even met you before?"

"A few years back, Rodney took me to meet you, but when we got there, you were asleep. And there were no other times that he made it possible for us to meet," I explained.

"But you said y'all been off and on for over three years. So I guess y'all were on, since you are pregnant." She shook her head and didn't give me a chance to respond. She then said, "I love my son, and I knew he was a man that didn't want to be with just one woman. But this situation right here," she said, pointing to my stomach, "we're gonna have to get a blood test. He already has too many kids out here to count on one hand. I know that I will have to care for them now since he's . . . gone," Ms. Roberts said bluntly. My heart fell to my stomach. A lady called Ms. Roberts's name, and before she turned and walked away, she huffed and said, "We'll talk later, child." I just watched as she walked away.

"Melody, don't mind my mother. She can be a little feisty and rude at times. But if you need anything, just let me know. Take care of yourself for the baby's sake." Tasha gave me a hug.

"Thanks," I said as we departed. Then I walked alone to my car.

42

Asia

When I woke up in the morning, I didn't get a chance to ask Steve what the hell he was doing that he didn't make it home until three in the morning. He was already gone to work when I opened my eyes. I slept in because I was tired from the long night I had with Melody and trying to comfort her in her time of mourning. I was shocked that she'd been hiding her pregnancy. I was going to have to call her after I got done working.

It would've probably been a good idea to take her out for dinner so she could've gotten out of the house to relieve some stress. I knew how much she loved that man, and for him to die in such a tragiclike way, I knew she was devastated. I just hoped she would be able to get over his passing in a timely matter for her daughter's sake. And she really didn't need to be stressed while she was pregnant.

I got in my car to go and show a home to a new client. As I got comfortable in my seat, I looked down on the front passenger's seat and noticed a man's belt buckle that evidently fell off of a belt. Steve had my car out late last night, but I hadn't ever seen that belt buckle before. I didn't notice it when I went by Melody's house. I picked it up and put it in my purse; I was going to ask Steve about it when I got home.

I had gotten a call yesterday from a lady that was very excited to see this spacious, two-story, four-bedroom, two-bath, Colonial-style home. It was a newly remodeled home on the east side of town, sitting on five acres of land. The listing price was $90,000. I told her I would meet her there at noon. I forgot to set my alarm clock, but I didn't think I was going to sleep past ten. I was beat. I made it to the house at eleven fifty; I was glad to see that she hadn't arrived yet. I could get my pitch together and look over the house to see what it had to offer so that I could explain it better to my client. I did a quick walk-through of the home.

"Okay, it has a beautiful coffered ceiling in the dining area, dark wood flooring throughout the house, and large windows," I said to myself.

After that, I walked into the kitchen and saw the dual wall oven, the light granite counters, and the large island. I checked out the bedrooms on the second floor. The tray ceiling in the master was gorgeous, and the large, outdoor, screened-in deck was to die for. I hoped that the client would fall in love with it. But I knew how to work my magic, so after I finished hyping the place up, she would want to close on the house immediately.

After about twenty minutes passed, I heard a car pulling up on the gravel in front of the house. I walked to the front door, and that's when I was stunned into silence. Lance was standing on the porch, holding a knife in his right hand. I was so shocked that I didn't move. My feet were stuck where I stood. He grabbed my arm and yanked it so hard that it felt like he jerked it out of its socket. He dragged me by my arm through the dining area to the kitchen. He then threw my body against the kitchen wall like I was a rag doll, and my head thumped hard against it.

"Ouch!" I said as I grabbed my aching head.

"So, we meet again." He gave me a sinister grin. "This is a nice house," he said as he looked around the large gourmet kitchen fit for a king and his queen. "This would've been a perfect house for us—but, no, you had to go and marry that prick husband of yours. Did he ever tell you that he and I have bumped into each other?" He smirked.

I couldn't believe what he was saying. He met Steve? When? Where? Did Steve already know about the relationship that I had with Lance? Was he keeping it to himself until I told him?

I didn't believe what Lance was saying. Maybe he was just trying to scare me.

"How do you know my husband?" I glared at him.

"Don't worry your pretty little self about how your husband and I know each other. Just know that we have met on *many* different occasions. But enough about him. By the way, you *are* looking good since you lost all that extra fat that you were carrying around. I put this meeting together so I could tell you that . . . and if you don't get your act together, I'm going to have to tell your husband that you and I are still sleeping together."

"That's a lie, and you know it. My husband's not going believe a liar like you," I spat.

"Shut up," he said and smacked me hard across my face. My face flung to the right due to the force of the blow.

How did I get myself in this situation? All I did was care about him while we were in a relationship; then I broke it off with him because I wanted to move on. Yet, there he was, torturing me every chance he got.

"What do you want from me?" I cried out.

"You know what? That is a *damn* good question. I don't want you because you're a whore, and you can't be trusted. I trusted you, and you were playing me like a sucker. I never would have thought that you would get back with your ex after he got out of jail. I thought our bond was strong, and you let that dude interfere with what we had going on like I was nothing to you. I just want to . . . um . . . make your life a living hell." He gave me another sinister grin. He was still holding on to the knife.

"Lance, I cared for you too. It was hard to break the news to you. But I rekindled the relationship with him because we have a child together, and my daughter really needs her father in her life," I pleaded.

"Didn't I tell you to shut up?" He smacked me across my face again. That time, I lost my balance and fell to the floor. "I didn't tell you to talk, and I didn't tell you to bring up that lame-ass dude in our conversation. You're just using your kids as scapegoats. You really don't care about them kids. You were never there for them; you were always with me. You always left them alone and let them fend for themselves. You are so full of shit, and I don't want to even look at you any longer." He was enraged.

His face was dark with fury, as if he was about to lose it. He came toward me with the knife and lifted it. I screamed out in fear. I knew he was about to kill me, but then, I heard a loud *thump,* and Lance moaned out in pain. I opened my eyes as he fell to the floor, and that's when I saw Steve standing over Lance holding a large cast-iron skillet that he used to hit Lance over the head with.

"Steve! Oh my God! He was trying to kill me," I shouted as I got up and hugged him. He hugged me for a quick second. I could tell he was also pretty shaken up from what had just happened. I wondered how in the world he knew where I was. But however he knew, I was glad he did because he'd saved my life. Lance was crazy, and I wished I would've known that before I got too close to him because I would've cut him loose a long time ago.

After Steve released himself from our embrace, he got down on his knees to check Lance's pulse. His body was still, and at that moment, I realized that he had not moved at all after he fell to the ground.

"Oh, no. Is he dead?" I asked as I shook my head. My body was soaked from perspiration. Lance was a small man, and his size didn't compare to Steve's bodybuilder, muscular frame at all.

Steve looked at me with sorrow in his eyes and said, "Yes."

43

Sasha

I still couldn't believe that fool had me smoking weed laced with crack cocaine. And at that very moment, I sat in my home and thought about how I felt when I hit the joint. I kinda knew something wasn't right, but I just thought it was me because I hadn't smoked in a long time. Besides, I had heard people talk about how potent the good weed could be. I never in a million years thought I was smoking that shit that could get me hooked. I needed to make sure I kept my mind at ease because I didn't want to be looking for a dealer to give me more of the drug. I was definitely done with Lamel. I was partying way too hard and doing way too much. *Did we even use protection last night?* I shook my head. What the hell was wrong with me? I was acting like a high school girl with no responsibilities. I had to get myself together before I lost it. I had too much going on for me to let a man bring me down with partying, sex, and drugs.

I was going to start planning for my book launch party, and I wanted it to be fabulous. I was a new author, coming out with the heat, and I wanted to make sure all my ducks were in a row. I didn't want to half step nothing. I knew I was under a publishing company, but I knew I still had to grind and find my audience. I knew that I had to still promote and grind because nobody was going to put my work out like I would. I wasn't playing when I said that I wanted my book to be on the big screen one day. But for that to happen, I had to get out and get noticed for the work that I did.

There was a lot of stuff going on, though. Melody had called me and told me that Rodney had gotten shot, but she thought he would pull through. But then she called back about a week later and said that he had passed away. I had gone over to her house the night before the funeral, and she was a mess. I felt so sorry for her and the baby that she was keeping a secret. But I really felt bad for Rayn. Melody wasn't giving that child the time and love that she needed because she was busy grieving Rodney. I knew how it felt not to have a parent there to show affection. I just hoped that Melody got it together soon before her daughter suffered from what was going on.

When I went over, Rayn answered the door because Melody was closed up in her dark bedroom. I tried to make small talk with Rayn, but she didn't want to talk. She looked depressed and sad. I told her that if she needed anything that she could call me anytime. She didn't say a word; she just nodded her head.

When I opened up Melody's bedroom door, she was slouched down in her bed, wrapped in her housecoat, staring at the wall. When we talked, she sounded as if she was struggling to say her words. She was weak, her eyes were red and puffy, and her hair was matted to her head. I could smell the stench from her breath from where I sat on her bed. I told her that she really needed to get up and tend to her daughter. But instead of answering me with words, she moaned. I was really concerned with her well-being. I was going to have to do something about it, and the only thing I could think about doing that would help was to call her mother and tell her to come down here and stay with her. My aunt always knew how to bring a person out of the slumps. She was heavily religious, and she would pray all your pain away.

"Come on, Melody, you need to get up. Let me make you something to eat," I said as I pulled open her curtains to let the sunlight lighten up her gloomy room.

"I'm not hungry."

"Well, that baby is. As a matter of fact, when do you go to the doctor? I'll go with you."

"I don't know," she said and pulled the covers over her head.

I tried so hard, but she wouldn't get out of the bed. I made her and Rayn a pot of spaghetti; then I left. But as I walked to my car, I called my aunt to tell her that she needed to come and see about her daughter. When I got a hold of her, she had some disturbing news for me.

"Sasha, I was just about to call you," my aunt said in a panic.

"What's up, Auntie?" I said nervously because her voice didn't sound right.

"Your mother's in the hospital."

"What happened to her? Is she going to be all right?" I cried out. I pulled over onto the side of the road. I was thinking the worst, and I didn't want to be the one to cause an accident.

"She'll make it. She ran in front of a car, and the car hit her. She broke one of her ribs and one of her legs."

"She ran in front of a car? Why? What was going on?"

"She said someone was chasing her, but there were witnesses out there when it happened, and they said that she was not being chased by anyone. I don't know why she would do that. We are all baffled," my aunt said.

"Well, tell her I'm on my way up there. I'll be there in about an hour." I hung up before she could say another word, swerved my car back on the road, and headed to Michigan.

***

When I got to the hospital, my mother was happy to see me. But I was sad to see her all banged up and bruised because I had a feeling I knew the reason why she was the way she was.

"Hi, Mom." I walked up to her and kissed her on the cheek. I didn't want to hug her because I didn't want to hurt her.

"Hey, sweetie." She gave me a half smile. She looked so uncomfortable. Her face was swollen, and her body was all bandaged up.

"Mom, tell me what happened." I sat on the edge of her bed and looked into her eyes.

"I don't remember. I don't remember how I got hit by that car." She was short with her words. She kept batting her eyes as if she was falling asleep. The nurse had told me that they had just given her some pain medicine.

"The nurse told me that there were people outside when the accident occurred. They said that they watched you as you ran down the block. They said that it seemed that you were running from someone and screaming, telling them to leave you alone. But there was no one following."

"I said I don't remember," she spat out in anger. We were silent for a while. "I'm sorry. I didn't mean to scream at you. It seems like I'm losing my mind. First, you told me about the horrible things I did to you as a child; then I get fired from job after job because my employers think I'm crazy, and now—this. I'm sitting in the hospital and can't remember a damn thang." Tears rolled down her cheeks. "I'm just so tired."

"Mom, I think that doctor you talked to in the past was telling you the truth. You may be schizophrenic. Please, can you get a second opinion? I don't want anything like this to happen to you again." I took her hand and cuffed it in mine.

She nodded her head as she wiped her eyes with the Kleenex I gave her. We talked for a while, and I was stunned that she didn't fall asleep because she looked so tired. She asked me what was going on in my love life. I told her that I had just gotten out of a relationship. She wanted to hear more, so I told her about how Lamel and I got down. Well, I didn't go over *all* the details, but when I was done talking to her, she responded by saying that every woman needed a young man that liked to be spontaneous and carefree. Every woman needed a young man to bring excitement to the relationship. She was so giddy when we talked about my relationship. She said she hadn't been in a relationship in years because men didn't understand her.

While I was sitting and talking to my mother, I couldn't help but to think about the irritation and burning feeling I was getting whenever I urinated now. I was thinking that since I was here in the hospital, I should walk down to the ER and get checked out. I figured it was just a bacterial infection. I was very sensitive and seemed to always contract infections.

After my mom finished her dinner, she told me to turn on the news. She never missed the news or *Wheel of Fortune*. When I flipped through the channels, I was shocked to see the news broadcaster talking about a death on the west side of Toledo. There was always stuff going on and people killing people. But I was shocked because Asia and Steve were talking on the news about some lunatic that was stalking Asia.

They said that Steve killed a man in self-defense. Asia held her head low and never looked into the camera. The only way people watching knew it was her was because her name was on the bottom of the screen. I couldn't believe my ears. *Steve killed someone? Wow. Someone was stalking Asia!* Then, the deceased's mug shot was up on the screen. That face looked familiar, but I couldn't remember where I'd seen him. I squinted my eyes to focus and thought a little harder.

"Oh my God!" I gasped. *That's the man that I saw kissing Asia's husband, Steve, in the parking lot at their wedding.*

44

Melody

I lay in bed, contemplating my next move. I didn't have the energy to move, but I knew that I had to do something because I had a daughter and a baby growing inside me that needed me. Sasha had made Rayn and me spaghetti, and she stayed awhile, preaching to me about how I needed to get out of my room and tend to my daughter. She was right, but I couldn't stop crying, and my heart wouldn't stop aching from the pain and emptiness I felt knowing that Rodney was never coming back to me.

I kept having flashbacks of us together. I thought about the times I would go to the YMCA and watch him play basketball with his boys. I loved to see his sexy, sweaty, muscular body dribbling the ball down the court before shooting a three-pointer, and then looking over at me and smiling. I would be on the bleachers cheering him on.

I reminisced about the times we went to the club together and how he would nibble on my ear and whisper sweet nothings in it. I remembered the times we would go out to eat at fancy restaurants, and he would order food that I thought I wouldn't like. I would tell him I wasn't going to eat it; then he would feed it to me, and I would fall in love with the entrée like I fell in love with him the very first time I tasted his lips.

Images flooded my mind of all the great sex we had. My body melted every time I felt him inside of me. He was always so gentle with me. He yearned to make me feel good, and he pleased me every time. He always made me feel sexy. I was in heaven when he touched me, and his caring hugs would uplift me out of any bad situation I was going through at that time. Oh, how I wished he could embrace me in his arms now. I was going to miss the texts I would get from him every day. He would text me good morning in the a.m. and good night when he knew I was on my way to bed—even if he was out late gambling.

I pulled out my photo album that I'd made just for Rodney and me. In all the pictures, we looked so in love and happy. As I flipped through the book, I saw the pictures of us at Cedar Point. I had a fear of riding roller coasters, but I got on the Magnum anyway—and I got sick to my stomach, and we had to leave early. He wasn't mad that we had to cut our fun date short; he just wanted to make sure I felt better.

I turned the page and saw a photo of us with my aunt, mother, and Rayn together at this soul food restaurant. We were there, celebrating Rodney and Ryan's birthday, which was on the same day. We had taken a dozen pictures at the club that I had kept for memory's sake. Now, that's all he is to me.

A memory.

Rodney was my better half; he was the one that I was going to marry. Yes, we had our ups and downs, but I knew that one day, he would come around and see that I was the one that he needed in his life forever. He introduced me to so many things in life. We talked about everything. We comforted each other when needed. I could be myself around him. We laughed, and we cried together.

There were some things that I just didn't understand about him, but maybe it wasn't meant for me to understand. No one was perfect; we both had things that we needed to work on. But now that he was gone, I wished that I could have at least said good-bye to him. I wished I could have hugged him one last time. And the fact that I didn't was eating me alive. I was mad at my beautician for not getting me out of the salon on time to see him one last time. But I was also mad at Rodney for leaving me in this world alone and heartbroken.

Before Sasha left, she turned on the radio since I lied and told her I couldn't find the remote for my TV. Jennifer Hudson belted out the lyrics to "Where You At?" *"You said you'd be there for me."* With each verse, I felt a connection with the song. That song represented what Rodney and I had and what he told me on a daily basis. I was pacing the floor, listening to the song. My emotions were all fucked up, and I was on my way to the radio to turn it off when Jennifer sang, *"You said you'd be there for me boy when the tough got going."*

"Rodney, why . . . Why did you have to be there at that club? Rodney, why didn't you sit yo' ass down like the doctors told you to? Why . . . why . . . why!" I shouted out until my voice went hoarse. I knew my neighbors heard me, but I didn't care. My knees became weak, and I fell to the floor and cried my brains out.

After the song went off, I didn't have the energy to walk to the bathroom that was only about three feet from where I sat, so I crawled on my hands and knees, and once I entered, I lifted my butt to the toilet seat. Weakly, I turned to look in the medicine cabinet to find some pain pills to knock the headache out that I had. I didn't see anything that would help my agony, but then, I looked on the basin of the sink, and I saw the razor blade that I had used to arch my eyebrows.

I picked it up and looked at it for a moment. The sharpness of it and how it shined under the light gave me a high of some sort. Maybe that was just what I needed. Pain pills wouldn't have lasted long enough, but in my mind, at that very moment, that blade would take me out of my misery. I placed the blade diagonally against my thin wrist and stared at all the veins that popped out at me. I then closed my eyes.

My mind was blank, and I wasn't thinking about anyone. Not Rayn, not my unborn child, and not my family. My hand shook unsteadily as I pressed the blade into my skin. And that was when I heard a cry. "Mom!" I opened my eyes quickly, and there was Rayn, standing in the doorway of the bathroom with tear-filled eyes. She had her hand up to her mouth in shock.

I immediately dropped the blade, which fell into the sink. That's when I saw the blood on my skin. I gasped out from the sight, but then I called out for Rayn. "Baby, please . . . I . . . I . . ." I stuttered as Rayn ran out of the bathroom. I didn't know what to say. I couldn't believe that my daughter had seen me in that state of mind.

45

Asia

Was I having a nightmare? I couldn't believe that Lance had tried stab me. He had put someone up to calling to view a home; then he came and clowned on me. But I was shocked to see Steve come to my rescue. He told me that he had followed me because he wanted to surprise me with flowers to make up for the argument we had the night he came home late. But he had noticed that I was in the home too long, and that's when he invited himself in, and I'm so glad that he did. But I didn't know that it would end the way it did. Lance, my ex-lover, was dead, and my husband killed him.

"Okay, what we are going to do is . . . Umm, I need you to call nine-one-one and tell them that you were being stalked by this man, and I came up to protect you because you told me someone was following you on your way up here." He breathed in, then said, "No, you can just tell them the truth, that I followed you up here because I wanted to surprise you. I had no clue that this bum, Lance, was going to be here."

"Okay, let me get my phone." I reached into my purse and did what I was told.

The police came out and asked us again what happened. I didn't even catch it when Steve mentioned Lance's name when we were talking. So Lance was right; he *did* know him. I was going to ask him about the connection later when we got home.

The news got wind of the death and came out to interview us. The police sealed off the house until they investigated everything. The whole scene happened so fast; I just hoped that Steve didn't get arrested. I couldn't wait for it all to be over so I could go home to my kids.

When I got home, I cooked dinner and tried to ease my mind. Since I didn't know how to cook many different meals, I stuck with what I knew best. I baked some pork chops, green beans, corn on the cob, and biscuits. I just wanted to sit at the dinner table and eat with my family. I was grateful to be alive.

I told the kids briefly about what had happened; I didn't want to go into great detail, but I did want to tell them something before someone else told them because it was all over the news. After we ate, I tucked my kids into bed and told them that I loved them. After I got them settled, I got in the shower and let the hot water caress my tense body. I just thought about all the drama I was having in my life. I needed to get out and get a drink—something I knew was a stress reliever.

When I got out of the shower, I checked my phone because I heard it beep, letting me know that I had a text message. I checked the message. It was from Sasha. She wanted to know if I wanted to join her and Melody for dinner on Saturday. *Is hell freezing over?* Sasha was actually contacting *me*. I replied and said sure. Maybe she was finally going to be mature enough to accept my apology so we could move on.

After I sent the text, I put on my nightwear and sat on the bed where Steve was sitting up watching the football game. I was glad that he wasn't asleep because I needed some questions answered.

"Steve, how did you know that guy?"

He gave me a confused looked that said "what guy?" I knew he wasn't about to play games with me. "You're talking about the dude that you were messing around with?"

"I wasn't messing around with him . . . Well, I was seeing him when you were locked up. But then, when you got out, I told him that I had feelings for someone else," I said. When I looked at him, his eyes were wide with shock.

"So, it was true; you two *were* together. Why didn't you tell me?" he wanted to know.

"He told me that he would kill all of us. And to this day, I still don't understand why he treated me like he did. I guess he was just plain ol' crazy." I shook my head and looked over at Steve. He was silent. "You still haven't told me how you knew him."

"I told you I didn't know him," he said without giving me eye contact.

"So, how did you know his name?"

"What are you talking about?"

"When you were trying to put an alibi together after you knocked him out, you said his name."

"No, I didn't." He became fidgety.

"Yes, you did. I heard what you said." I was becoming agitated.

"Well, maybe I said his name because I heard you say his name when I was in the dining room listening to you two argue," he said.

"So why didn't you just say that from the get-go?" I wanted to know. I could tell that Steve was hiding something from me, and I was going to get to the bottom of it.

"Asia, this has been a very stressful day. I just forgot. That's all," he said as he picked up the remote, clicked the TV off, and lay down on the bed, leaving me sitting up in the dark.

Maybe I was making a big deal out of nothing. He did just kill a man. I knew he was stressed out. I crawled into bed, and as soon as my head hit the pillow, I was out. I was exhausted, and I needed that rest.

46

Melody

My mother was a lifesaver. She came down after Sasha told her that I needed her. But Rayn's father was another story altogether. I couldn't believe what he was trying to put me through. If it wasn't for my mother being by my side, I probably would've been in jail for murdering my baby's daddy.

As I sat down and revisited the moment when Cedrick, Rayn's father, came in my house, trying to take my daughter from me, I got enraged all over again.

"Melody, what the hell is going on? Rayn called me crying hysterically last night," Cedrick boomed after I opened the door. I looked him up and down with my nose turned up. Then, I walked away, leaving him standing there, looking like a fool. He continued ranting. "What is going on with you for my daughter to be up in here while you were trying to harm yo' self?" He paused and waited for an answer.

I turned around quickly. "I . . . I was going through a lot, and I was stressed, but I wasn't going to do anything stupid." I couldn't look him in the eyes because I was lying. I still felt horrible about what I had allowed Rayn to see.

"Please don't tell me what Rayn said was true. Were you *really* gonna slice yo' wrist?" He walked closer to me. I swallowed the lump that was forming in my throat as my heart thumped against my chest.

Why did people continue to bring that up? I was sick of hearing it. "I *said* I wasn't gonna do nothing stupid," I snapped.

"Who do you think you're fooling? You can't even look me in the eyes. I *know* you're lying," he snapped back.

"Look, I don't have to explain a got-damn thing to you." I walked away from him, hoping that the conversation was over. I slouched down on the sofa with an attitude that screamed *leave me the hell alone!* I wanted him to leave before I got heated. I was *not* in the mood to be criticized by my baby's daddy.

"You *do* have to explain, especially if you've got my daughter around this crazy shit. You think it's all right that she's so messed up because she thinks her mother doesn't want to live. She thinks that you were trying to kill yourself. She said that you have been closed up in your room and not giving her any attention," he bellowed in his deep voice as he stood over me.

My body shook from the bass in his voice and from the words that he said. Tears formed behind my lids as the memory of that night flooded my mind. My poor baby; I probably ruined her for life. "Cedrick, I really don't feel like talking right now. Did you come her to take Rayn out to dinner or something?" It would've been nice for Rayn to get some fresh air to get her mind off of everything that had been going on.

"As a matter of fact, yes . . . I came to get Rayn, but we'll be doing more than having dinner. Melody, I'm going to take her with me. I think that, right now, my home is more stable for her."

I glared at him. "Oh, okay. You can have her for the weekend. She would enjoy that."

"No, Melody. I ain't talking about just for the weekend. I'm going to take her to live with me until you get yourself together—however long that may take." He took a few steps back from me and interlocked his hands in front of him.

"You've got to be shitting me. You *really* think I'm going to let you take my daughter?" I stood up and jabbed my finger in his face as I spoke to him, venom lacing my voice. "Rayn has been *my* priority ever since she was born. If you think you're gonna come up in here and take her from me, you better think again. Just because I had a little fuckup doesn't mean I'm not a good mother. I would never harm my daughter. I want you to go *now!*" That man hadn't spent quality time with Rayn in who knows how long. He was the type of father that would buy whatever was needed to keep her happy, but he barely spent time with her. Now he was trying to act like he was father of the year. It was time for him to dismiss himself with that bullshit.

"Melody, I'm not leaving without her. I just want to—"

"Oh, you *are* going to get the hell out of here, and Rayn will *not* be going with yo' ass." I walked over to the door and opened it. That was when I saw my mother standing there.

"Um . . . Hey, Mom," I said in shock. I didn't know she was coming to visit.

"Hey, Melody," she said as she walked in and gave me a tight hug. From the way she looked at me and from the way she held me in her arms, I knew that she knew what was going on with me. I didn't know how much she knew, but she knew something.

"Hi, Ms. Dickson," Cedrick said as he walked over to give my mother a hug.

I cleared my throat. "Oh, yeah, Mom, gon' 'head and get yo' little hug from him because he was on his way out." I rolled my eyes and motioned for Cedrick to get to stepping.

I wished it was that easy, but it wasn't. He pulled my mother to the side and told her what Rayn told him and that he wanted to take her for a while. But my mother talked to him and asked if he could just take her for the weekend because she wanted to see her while she was in town. He agreed. After he left, my mother and I sat down and talked about the hell my life had been over the past few weeks.

"Melody, I'm so sorry that you lost the man that you loved so dearly. I know you're hurting, but you have to get it together, baby. You have to be strong. You have a daughter that is watching you. You are her provider. She looks up to you, and she loves you to death. If something would happen to you, what do you think that would do to her?" My mom pleaded with me with her eyes.

Tears formed in my own eyes, blocking my vision. "Mom, I didn't plan to get that razor out. I don't know what I was thinking. I . . . I just wanted the pain to go away. I know that was a stupid thing to do because Rayn is my heart, and I would never want her to see me like that. I'm so stupid," I cried out. My heart ached from mourning the loss of Rodney and for disappointing my daughter.

"Baby, it's going to be okay. I will stay here with you until you get over this thing. Your emotions are all crazy because you are pregnant. I promise things will get better. You have to get back in a positive state of mind so that you can have a healthy baby." Mom held my head close to her chest as she talked to me.

I lifted my head and looked into her eyes. "I didn't even get to say good-bye to him. I couldn't even see him for the last time. Once I got to the funeral, the casket was closed." I blinked out more tears.

"Baby, maybe it wasn't meant for you to see him like that. Maybe God wanted you to remember him the way he was when you last saw him alive. You know that it's not good to see a corpse while you're pregnant."

I just shook my head. She couldn't understand the pain I was going through because she wasn't me. I was done talking about it. I knew I had to get it together for my kids . . . but how? How was I going to get over the fact that I would give birth to a fatherless child?

47

Sasha

I didn't want to leave my mother at home to care for herself, but after a week, I had to get home and get back to work. She was doing much better. Even though she was still healing from her accident, she was able to get around in her home okay, and she looked good. She had decided to see a doctor for her schizophrenia. I was shocked that she didn't take it too hard, but I knew deep down that she knew she was ill. I'm just glad that she was no longer in denial, and she was about to start her treatment process. They gave her medications, and so far, her body reacted well to it.

I brought my laptop with me so that when she was resting, I could work on my novel. Being signed to a publishing company was very rewarding, but it could also be very stressful because I had to meet deadlines. I had to work and take care of everything around my house, and even on days that I was tired, I still had to get my word count in. I'm glad I didn't have kids because that would be a lot to balance. I thought I had a whole lot of stories in my mind, but as I wrote this second book, I was getting writer's block. I would sit at my computer and think hard about what I should write. I did outlines for each chapter, but I only outlined the action parts of the chapter. It was becoming tough for me to fill in the paragraphs with things that would come before and after the action.

My editor was a lifesaver. Even though we had never met because we lived in different states, we really connected over the phone. She helped me better myself as a writer. She would tell me where I needed to improve, and I would try to work on what she pointed out. If it wasn't for her, I would have lost my mind. But when I was feeling frustrated, she would read a scene in my book, and then ask me what I think needed to be done. That helped me out so much because, after hearing someone else read my work to me, I could envision what needed to be changed.

I turned the key to the door of my apartment. After being gone for a week, I walked into a mess trap. I must have had food in the garbage because once I smelled the stench from the kitchen, I wanted to pass out. I had stuff everywhere because I had rushed to be by my mother's side after my aunt told me she was in the hospital. I pulled the trash bag out of the can, tied it up, and walked it out to the Dumpster. Then, I emptied my suitcase and put a load of clothes in the washer. I wasn't in the cleaning mood, but I managed to get the dust mop and rag and went to work. As I was cleaning. I felt my phone vibrating in my pocket.

"Hello."

"Damn, girl, are you coming or not? We're hungry," Melody whined.

Oh my God! I had seriously forgotten about our dinner date. "Girl, I'm on my way, but y'all can go ahead and order. I'm leaving home now." I hung up and didn't give her time to respond because I knew she was going to have a fit that I wasn't close.

As I walked into the restaurant, I saw that both Melody and Asia were digging into their food. I was also happy that the restaurant wasn't too packed, which meant it wouldn't take long for me to get my order in.

"Dang, y'all heffas could've waited for me," I smiled as I took my seat at the table.

"Girl, gon'. I told you we were ready to eat. What took you so long anyway?" Melody wanted to know.

"When I got back from Michigan, I decided to start cleaning because my house was a mess, and it slipped my mind that we had a dinner date," I confessed. I picked up the menu to see what I wanted to order. I loved Ruby's Kitchen; they had the best soul food in town. I decided to order the fried catfish and fried potatoes and onions.

"How is Aunt Arlene doing?" Asia asked as she stuffed a forkful of food in her mouth.

"Yeah, is she recovering well?" Melody asked.

"She's doing okay. She still has pain every so often, but after she takes her pills, she's fine. She was diagnosed with schizophrenia."

"Wow," was all Melody said with sympathy in her eyes.

"What!" Asia said with wide eyes. I had never told her about how my mom treated me as a child, so she had no clue.

"Is there a cure for that?" Melody wanted to know.

"She's taking medication that will help her body cope better with the disorder. There are many people that live long and healthy lives. I think she'll be fine. But I'll take more trips to see her. I'm just glad she's now receiving the medications that she needs."

We talked a little more about my mother; then Asia started talking about the situation she was in. She was telling us that her ex-boyfriend was stalking her and peeping in her windows; then she admitted that he was the same guy that Steve killed to protect her. I was in shock to know that the man that was killed was the same man that she was with because she never introduced us to him. But he *was* the same guy that I saw Steve kissing at her wedding. I needed to let her know because that whole situation was fucked up.

"Asia, I've got something to tell you. I know you are about to be mad at me, but I think that it's time for me to tell you something that I knew about your husband from day one," I said as I took a sip of well-needed vodka from my glass.

She glared at me as if she was saying, *"Heffa, if you've been holding something foul from me, I'm going to whip yo' ass!"*

I took another sip of my drink and told her my truth. "The day of your wedding, I saw your husband kissing a man in the parking lot in broad daylight," I spit out.

Melody choked on her food and took a sip of her water. Then she stared at me before turning to look at Asia.

Asia was silent as she looked deep into my eyes, almost as if she was trying to set me on fire with hers.

"You know, back then, we were feuding, and I didn't care to tell you what I knew. I kinda took it as payback for you setting me up with a man that you had dealt with in the past. You knew you were wrong for that, and I was wrong for keeping this from you. But when I saw that the man on the news was the one that your husband kissed, and then killed, I had to tell you. So, I guess . . . you know . . . You can say that we're even." I gave her a little smirk that said that there was no love lost. We were now cool.

The next thing I knew, I was picking my face up off of the floor. It all happened so fast. Asia got up from her seat and punched me hard, straight in the jaw. I fell back in my seat and hit the floor. She had a mean punch for a white girl. I stood from the floor after Melody helped me up and rubbed my jaw where it stung.

Melody looked me dead in the eyes and said, "You wrong for that shit." Then she walked off leaving me standing there.

Yes, I could admit that I deserved that. I looked around to see if Asia was going to attack me again because I wanted to be ready. But she was long gone. I didn't see her and me ever having a trustworthy relationship again like we had when we were growing up. Our relationship was damaged beyond repair. But I still cared for her, and I wondered what she was going to do with that low-down, on the down low, husband of hers.

48

Asia

I would never have thought that Steve, or my cousin, would deceive me like they did. Sasha and I grew up together. We weren't blood, but we were cousins. Yes, we had our issues in the past. I was mad at her for marrying my first crush, so I hooked her up with a guy that I had slept with. I truly didn't think she was going to bang him; after all, she was a married woman. But she stooped to the lowest level when she sat there and watched me marry the man that she saw, just moments before, kissing a man.

I was so livid with her when she told me that at the restaurant. My heart stopped, and my mind went blank. But then, memories reeled through my mind of all the things that I had done to help Steve out when he got released from prison. I was so angry about how he deceived me. While I sat there and thought about the things we had been through and the stuff that Lance had done to me, Sasha continued to talk as if what she had done was cool because it was "payback" for me. I was tired of her mouth, so I punched her in her jaw to shut her up. She fell backward in her chair. She blacked out, I don't know for how long because I got up and left. That trick was crazy, and I had nothing else to say to her.

When I got home to face my so-called husband, he tried to play like he was so innocent.

"Babe, what are you talking about? I never saw that dude in my life," he said after I confronted him. I lied and told him that someone told me that they had seen him and Lance out together.

But when I hit him with, "Steve, did you kiss Lance in the parking lot of the church on the day of our wedding?" it looked as if he was going to pass out. Right then and there, I knew the answer. "Get yo' shit and get the fuck out of my house!" I screamed. "You filthy bastard. So you out here fucking men while you fucking me raw? Muthafucka, I will kill yo' ass!" I started throwing my fist at him as if I was hitting a punching bag. "I'm about to kill yo' ass!" That was when my son, Joey, came in the room, scared out of his mind.

"Mom, what are you doing? Why are you fighting with Dad?" he cried out.

All my kids had started calling him dad after we got married. That bastard wasn't no real man, and I had my kids looking up to him as a role model while he was out there screwing men. My blood boiled! All that time I was stressing myself out, and Steve knew Lance all along. What was really going on? I was disgusted, and I was hurt. I never thought in a million years that he would've done something so terrible to me on my wedding day. I wanted to know how they met. I wanted to know every-thing, but I wouldn't dare ask him. I wanted him out of my house—now.

"Joey, go to your room. Now!" I shouted, and he ran off.

I knew he was upset, but I would have to deal with him later. I couldn't even look at Steve. I didn't know who he was anymore. He was keeping a secret from me. The man I was running from was running into the arms of my husband. I was done with his ass. He had to go.

49

Melody

Four weeks later . . .

As I sat in the hospital, about to deliver my baby by C-section, I prayed to God that she would be okay. I was one month early because of toxemia. My blood pressure was high, so the doctor had to schedule a C-section. I was about to bring another life in the world, another little girl, so I knew I had to stop being so naïve when it came to men. I knew it was going to be hard raising my daughter without her father, but I knew I was going to do the best I could. I didn't want to be in a relationship at that moment. I needed to be by myself to figure out what I needed, and I needed to give my undivided attention to my girls. Everyone was by my side, including Asia and Sasha—even though they weren't talking to each other. My mom held one hand, and Rayn held the other as we waited for the doctor to come in.

I had begun going to therapy to help me heal from Rodney's death. I was really learning a lot, and I was glad that I decided to go through with it because I was able to release a lot of stress. I loved my life, and I loved my daughter, and I didn't want to ever feel like I needed to end my life. I was in a much better place now.

274 No Perfect Affair

Asia had filed for divorce. I couldn't believe the mess she was in. I thought I was going through it, but Asia was going through much worse. After Steve killed the man that we found out he was kissing at their wedding, Asia also found out that he was having an affair with the man. I couldn't believe that Sasha knew, and she let Asia go on with her wedding. That was so foul; I would have punched her ass too.

After Asia put Steve out, she started going through his things, and she found letters Lance wrote Steve while he was still in jail. Asia found out that Steve and Lance were cool in jail; then, Steve got caught up and fell for Lance. But Steve had told Lance that what they did was a mistake, and when he got out of jail, he wanted to be with Asia.

Lance got released first, and that's when he approached Asia to get back at Steve. So, what Asia and Lance had was all a joke because Lance was mad and wanted to ruin Steve's life. In the process, he tried to hurt Asia because he was in love with Steve. Their love triangle was like one of those reality shows you see on TV. Did Lance really think he could have a perfect affair? I wonder why he just didn't tell Asia from the beginning that he was messing around with men. That down low crap was getting out of hand. I was so glad that Asia got herself out of that situation. I felt sorry for her kids; they loved that man. I shook my head as I thought about the things that men did to ruin a woman's life. Then, I thought about the things that women did to keep a man happy.

"Miss Dickson, are you ready to see your baby girl?" The doctor walked in the room.

I smiled and said, "Yes, I am, Doc."

He checked my vital signs; then I lay down in the hospital bed, and the nurses pushed me in to this big, cold, white room. My heart was beating at a fast pace;

I was so nervous. I had heard so many horrible stories about having a C-section.

"Melody, everything is going to be okay. I said a prayer for you, and I know God will keep you and my granddaughter safe," my mother said as she walked right beside me.

Charity was born at 11:53 a.m., weighing five pounds, six ounces. She was so beautiful with her caramel complexion and head full of curly, jet-black hair. Rayn fell in love with her, and she didn't want anyone else to hold her. Even though Charity was so small, she was a healthy baby, and she had no problems.

"I told you, baby, God was in the midst of it all," my mom told me after she saw that my baby and I were all right.

After a few days at the hospital, I was released. I was doing well, and I wasn't in much pain. When I got home, my mother stayed with me for a while. She didn't say it, but I knew that she was there to keep me sane because the doctor talked to her about postpartum depression. She didn't want me to fall back. I continued to go to counseling, and my life was great.

Rayn was also a big help to me. She made sure she asked me if I needed help any time she heard the baby crying. She was so mature for her age, and she was growing up to be so responsible.

Every time I looked into Charity's eyes, I couldn't help but to think about Rodney. She had his eyes and nose. I wished that he could see his beautiful daughter. I missed him so much.

After I healed from having my baby, I was ready to get back to work. I had run into an old friend I knew in college, and she told me that she knew someone leasing out a nice-sized space. She thought it would be perfect for my photography studio. I checked it out, and it *was* perfect. I would be moving into my new building in two weeks, and I couldn't wait.

I had some trials and tribulations in my life, but I was ready to stop looking back and move forward into my future with my two beautiful girls. I wanted them to be the best that they could be, and I had to be there to provide a safe environment for them. I loved my life, and I was going to be a great mother and a successful businesswoman.

The End

About the Author

Charmaine Galloway was born and raised in Toledo, Ohio. Writing has been her passion and a positive emotional outlet since middle school. As a teen, writing in her journal allowed her to escape the negativity of her world. Around that time she also began writing her first Christian fiction novel. She finds joy in creating unique and awe-inspiring story lines for the characters in her stories. Ingenuity and imagination are a mainstay and compass in her work.

Charmaine has been a guest on many blog talk radio shows and a featured author in *SORMAG's Digital, Urban Image, BlaqRayn,* and *Literary Lounge* magazines.

Titles by Charmaine include: *My World, Through My Eyes,* her debut poetry book. *Fulfill Your Dreams of Becoming a Self-Published Author,* her nonfiction book. *Girlfriends Secrets, The Secrets They Kept, Tyree's Love Triangle,* and *Golden* are her Amazon bestselling novels. *Heaven's Cry* and *Jordan's Confessions,* her short stories. *Girl Talk* and *Find The Princess Within* are her two inspirational books for teen girls. Charmaine has also written two children's books titled *I Love Myself As I Am* and *Mommy's Little Superhero.*

Ms. Galloway has a bachelor of arts in Family Life Education and an associate degree in Early Childhood Education. Becoming a fierce advocate and supporter of troubled young women has been a goal of hers since overcoming struggles of her own as a young woman. "I believe turning a blind eye or deaf ear to our struggling youth only promotes destruction and demise. They are human. They have a voice. You'll be surprised by what you can learn from them if you just listen."

Being the wearer of many proverbial "hats," Charmaine is a published author under Racquel Williams Presents (RWP) Publishing Company. Also, she is the founder of her own publishing company, Charming Gal Publications. She is the CEO and jewelry designer at Charming Gal Boutique (www.charmainggalboutique.com), her online jewelry boutique, and the owner of Amazing Grace Educational Childcare LLC (www.amazinggracechildcare.com). However, the most important "hat" she wears is that of Mom to her two children. Following her dreams as a writer and entrepreneur will leave a beautiful legacy for them by encouraging them to work hard to achieve their dreams because their mom didn't quit reaching for hers.

"As a new author, I think it is very important that my readers get to know me. I'm a writer with Christian values, and I hope to inspire people with the stories that I pen. My characters are everyday people going through struggles and obstacles because life is not perfect.

"With every story I create, there is a testimony that my characters will share about life and how they were transformed to become better people. Every story does not have a 'happily ever after' ending, and neither does real life."

Charmaine is currently working on new projects, so keep a lookout for her upcoming releases. Please visit www.charmainegalloway.com to check out her blogs and new blurbs.